The Princess of Cragside

Jo Priestley

The Women of Old Yorkshire Collection

For more information visit:
http://www.womenofoldyorkshire.com

ISBN   9798345616246

Other titles in the Women of Old Yorkshire collection:

Acknowledgements

I recall the precise moment when inspiration struck for this bittersweet tale of love: dusk, a New Year's Eve, and a trip to the historic Halifax *Piece Hall,* nestling beneath a craggy Pennine outcrop.

The hall, originally built for cloth trading in the 1700s, is now an enclosed square, surrounded by colonnaded shops and offices. A small building stands near the entrance which I thought would be the perfect place to live, with its ever-changing view of the crags through the seasons.

Much of this story is set in wintertime. I generally lean towards a cosy setting, even if my characters' lives are often less than comfortable.

Our late Queen, a woman dear to our hearts, plays an important part in the story when she was the Princess Elizabeth, but it was by chance that I later discovered the name of my leading lady, Bridie, means *Princess.*

I choose my character names carefully, ensuring they are appropriate for the setting and persona, but also as a way to keep the memory of loved ones alive. Her surname, Foxcroft, recalling a very dear friend, and the name of Bridie's best friend, Edyth, my mother-in-law.

My thanks to Andrew for his support; to Alana Jordan for the cover artwork; and to Ann, Janet, Sue and Tracey, my long-time reviewers, who believe in my writing so much and still spur me on.

A special thank you to Allie - a writer with many years of experience who took my little book and polished it … just because she cared so much about it. She really went above and beyond, and I will always be grateful.

And to Jax, a newcomer to my books, for all his enthusiasm and support.

Chapter 1

How powerful the man must have felt at that moment, holding all our lives in the palm of his hand. Elliott Frobisher sat glaring at the paperwork neatly stacked in front of him, giving nothing away.

His father's eyes scuttled across the faces around the boardroom table. He had clearly had some sleepless nights; the shadows making his stare appear even more intense. I had to look away.

"So, are we all in agreement?" he asked, his gaze finally settling on his son.

If truth be told, his son was the only person really being invited to answer the question because he was the only one dragging his feet. Oh, how he was revelling in his position.

Edyth and I exchanged glances, waiting and wondering if we would receive the answer we were hoping for, much the same as Mr Frobisher and the rest of the Board. Father and son's eyes locked suddenly, the look they shared making me very much doubt it. He was cutting his nose off to spite his face, as my mother would say, and I just happened to be the nose.

"Right, Elliott, listen carefully," Mr Frobisher said, failing to disguise the clear note of indignation in his voice. "I know it's a radical move, we all do, but if we don't make it, then we'll be up the proverbial creek without a paddle. *Frobisher's* will sink and all of us with it.

Now, I'm sure you wouldn't want that. You know well enough that we've been throwing good money after bad for years, so there's little of it left. If nothing else, think of your grandfather and the blood, sweat, and tears he shed to get us here and provide handsomely for his family."

He pointed a crooked forefinger in the direction of the oil painting above the marble fireplace, the one of Elliot Frobisher's grandfather wearing riding britches and boots. He holds the reins of his chestnut horse in one hand and a cigar in the other, looking a little smug, as well he might. It's fair to say that their ancestor was a fine-looking gentleman, a trait that runs in the family.

I searched for Edyth's hand under the table, grasping it tightly for reassurance when I found it. Mr Frobisher explained to me the previous day that board rules require unanimous agreement in the vote. There was so much at stake. I admit it stuck in my craw that our futures depended on one man agreeing to come on board with the plan.

The new doll samples were displayed in the middle of the boardroom table. They stared back at me, oblivious to the great debate unfolding around them. It always makes me smile to think that grown men are so invested in dolls, but then the Frobishers have made a good living from them. It was an extraordinary meeting of the Board and, along with the Frobishers, Edyth and I, were seated the company's investors who had travelled up from London. They generally come to see us quarterly, all perfectly turned out in their fine suits and expensive brogues, standing out like a sore thumb in these parts. They may as well have paid us a visit from the moon as they stride from the foyer to the lift that takes them to the top floor offices. They even smell differently, with their fancy colognes and hair tonics wafting about the factory; sometimes the aroma makes me a little nauseous as I prefer the scent of good, old-fashioned soap.

Mr Frobisher explained how timing was crucial as the new dolls had to be in shops in time for Christmas. Sales had already been tested at *Bradley's* toy shop in London, and much to Mr Frobisher's surprise and delight, they exceeded his expectations, he told me.

The time had come to place the dolls in regional department stores, and then eventually nationwide. He had taught me so much about the business, and in such a way I could understand, rather than being hoity toity and condescending.

Bradley's described the dolls as a 'much needed breath of fresh air', which boded well. It was a shot in the dark, but Mr Frobisher said drastic action had to be taken. There was no doubt my role at *Frobisher's* had changed, but still, the 'us' made my chest swell.

I would very much have liked to give his son a good shake. He was revelling in the moment and clearly finding satisfaction in keeping all of us on tenterhooks, for so many reasons. If he himself had come up with the idea, he would have been telling anyone who would care to listen how ingenious it was. Indignation made the hairs on the back of my neck creep like a cold draught had blown in. Edyth had been invited for moral support, and she squeezed my hand as I sat with my heart beating in my mouth. I closed my eyes briefly, enduring the torture of waiting for 'His Lordship' to agree to what was only sound business sense.

When I opened them, Elliott Frobisher was staring directly at me. His steely glare made my stomach drop, and from the corner of my eye I noticed Edyth and every Board member had followed the trail of his eyes to me. The silence was unnerving, so I tightened my grip on Briget's hand.

The glower that man was casting me across the boardroom table was nothing short of withering, and I could quite easily have wilted like a flower under the heat of it.

Worse still, the hateful spite in his narrowed eyes was telling all those important people that we had some sort of … connection.

Including—oh, the shame of it—his own father.

I still feel it to this day.

*

Home is often said to be a simple pleasure, yet for me, it is anything but.

I could never begin to unravel the many joys our little palace brings me; from the quiet contentment to the sense of safety, there are a million other little joys in between. I often think about it, as I know many people in the town are envious of our unusual circumstances.

Quiet contentment, however, has jumped to the head of the queue this evening, as it often does.

The quilt has been a true labour of love for my mother and me since October. This one is more elaborate, taking longer to sew as it's for the bed she shares with my father and it's already my favourite.

"We've waited far too long for a new quilt," she said as the nights began drawing in. "We always put ourselves last on the list, Bridie, and our room is in dire need of a lick and a polish."

The dainty stitching would pass muster with the most eagle-eyed seamstress, but then we've had plenty of practice between us over the years. It whiles away the evenings, and I know we both enjoy getting everything sorted after tea, then sitting down to make a start. Sewing and listening to the radio is always such a restful end to the day.

My mother is working now, head bowed, on a separate section of patchwork for them both to come together eventually as one. I've lost count of the quilts we've made since I was a child. Every special occasion calls for one from us—a wedding, a new home, a new baby—the town waits to see what we can produce between us. There's often a bag of old rags left on the step as if by magic when we come downstairs on a morning, and we put them to good use.

"I was offered that job at *Frobisher's*," I say, stretching to take another piece of fabric from the piles laid out neatly on the low table in front of us. "I feel as though I've been waiting forever for a vacancy to come up, and now they want me to start next week."

"Oh, I am pleased, Bridie," she says, taking off her glasses to look at me. "It will be lovely working with Edyth; you two have been like peas in a pod since you were children."

We have, it's true. All through school, we were inseparable, and she practically lives here. I see her every day still, despite me going to work at *Crossley's* mill instead. There was only one vacancy, and Edyth, being the elder of us, took it, which is only fair. Since then, she's been waiting for another one to come up for me so we could be reunited, and at last we will be. I prefer not to remember why, as it makes me gloomy, and feel as though I'm stepping into a dead woman's shoes. Alice Nutter was a sad loss for the company, but even more so as a friend and mentor to Edyth. She almost ran the shop floor during the war years and the other women greatly admired and respected her for it. She ran it with 'a bit of knowledge and a lot of commonsense' according to Edyth.

At least I'll still be working with my hands when I'm assembling the dolls. I find repetition soothing rather than tedious, so factory work will suit me down to the ground. It will certainly interest me far more than millwork, and I'm looking forward to a change.

"It's a job for life at *Frobisher's,*" my mother says now, getting up to stoke the flames of the fire. "The mill's the same, of course, but the fibres on your lungs get you in the end. I'm glad you're getting out, love, even if our Archie has to stay on." She smiles to herself now. "You'll almost be able to roll out of bed to the front door."

Sharing a chuckle, I admit it will be a bonus not to have to walk far, especially when the snow can cover your boots in Halifax much of the wintertime.

In truth, I'm not entirely sure it's as much a job for life as the mill. Edyth told me they're only replacing staff rather than hiring new ones, but I'll take the chance and not mention it to my mother or she'll only fret. It's a little dream come true of mine, so worth the risk, and if all else fails, I know they'll take me back at *Crossley's.* There's always room for workers there, as the mill is the 'bread and butter' of the town.

My mother and I sit quietly with the hum of the radio until the door opens to the wind, signalling the arrival of my father and brother, Archie, rolling home from the *Spitting Feathers*. I love the name of the pub; it comes from the wool fibres at the mill which look like feathers forever floating in the air.

"Here they are," my father says, stooping to kiss the top of my mother's head before grinning madly at her, full of beer.

Archie takes off his own coat then helps my father out of his before hanging them side by side on the coat stand by the door.

"Where else would we be?" my mother asks, the same as every night. The glow of the lamp highlights the tender look in her eyes, just another little routine that brings me comfort.

Usually this would be Archie's cue to tell us he's going to bed after rolling his eyes, but tonight he joins us by the fire instead. I look on with a fond smile as both men tussle to take their boots off. The demon drink is to blame, but these two daft articles are about as far from demons as a person could get.

"Honouring us with your presence tonight then, Archie," I say.

He gives up trying to remove his boots, flopping back on the settee.

"I am, and honoured you should be," he says, nudging me so I put down my sewing with a sigh. The peace of the evening blew out the front door into the wind of the night when they came through it.

He turns my way, then sits staring at me for so long I eventually realise he'd like to get something off his chest. It was the same when we were children, and just like then, I decide I should give him a helping hand.

"So, to what do we owe the pleasure?" I ask.

When he runs his hands over his hair, it sticks up like chapel hat pegs, the sight so endearing it twists my heart.

How I love my big brother. The pain I felt when he went to war was physical and is something that still follows me around. It was as though he was torn away, so I dread to think how our parents felt on that day. But they weren't the only ones, not by a long way.

Archie was too young to sign up when the war began, and I hoped it would be over before he was old enough, but I was to be disappointed. He returned in one piece and not terribly changed by the awful experience like some, so luck was on our side in the end, at least.

"I was just wondering," he looks away at the fire, "I've never heard you mention anything, so I was wondering," he shuffles in his seat but doesn't look my way, "I was wondering if Edyth is spoken for."

If my brother had told me he was running away to join the Foreign Legion, I could not have been more thrown by this enquiry after my friend's romantic life. I had no idea he was sweet on Edyth, and I doubt she has a clue either. The rest of us exchange glances, but my father looks unfazed, with a silly grin still on his face. Perhaps Archie had a word with him earlier to ask his thoughts on the matter.

I sit forward, turning to face my brother directly, so I make my position quite clear.

"Is this the drink talking, Archie? I don't think Edyth's name has ever passed your lips before now, even though you've known her forever the same as me. I have to say, I would hate you to mess her around."

His mouth hangs as he shakes his head repeatedly, trying to sit up straight in his seat.

"Bridie, I swear to you on my life that it isn't the drink that's moving my mouth." His face glows scarlet, a sure sign he must be speaking the truth if ever there was one. I can't think how to respond, so I sit quietly to ponder on his outburst.

"Is she though?" he asks eventually. He looks almost lovelorn, so I'm unable to recognise him as my confident brother. Sighing, I place a hand on his.

"No, she isn't spoken for, as you put it, Archie," I say. "That being said, I'm not sure how she feels about you, as this is all rather sudden, to say the least."

I'm startled when he grabs both my hands and I hear my mother gasp, wondering, I imagine, what could possibly have got into her son. My father is falling asleep in his chair already, unphased by the little drama happening only inches away.

"Will you … will you just put a good word in for me, that's all I ask, Bridie. Just test the water to see what she thinks about me before we go any further."

Test the water indeed. The last thing I want is to become involved in my brother's love life. He's walked out with quite a few local girls over the years and Edyth knows all about them. Edyth, however, most definitely isn't just any other girl.

"Archie, it's not for me to interfere. You need to ask her yourself; you're a big lad. The worst she can do is say no."

He leans forward now, dangling his hands between his legs.

"I know, but if she says no, then I'll still have to face her every time she comes here, and that's plenty."

His eyes are stretched when he looks at me from underneath his dark fringe, tugging my heartstrings further. The trouble with Archie is that he's too appealing for his own good, but to be fair to him, he doesn't let it go to his head. Not that his pals at the *Feathers* would ever let that happen.

"How much do you like her, lad?" My mother asks now. Her voice is so strangely quiet the simple question makes me look her way. Her eyes are fixed on her son, her face taut. I wonder why she seems so worried when nothing has happened yet.

Archie looks across at her now, saying, "A lot, mam, I like Edyth a lot."

They're speaking to each other in a way I don't understand at first, but as I study my brother's earnest expression, I suddenly realise why my mother is concerned: Her loyalties are torn between her two children for the first time.

Perhaps in her wisdom she knows if they should get together, and Archie should break Edyth's heart, then everything would change for all of us. She's become part of our family.

My cosy evening is suddenly spoiled as I look between my mother and brother. If Archie should let Edyth down, it won't be only one heart he's breaking.

Even more worryingly, I wonder if this time we would be able to find it in us to turn a blind eye and forgive him.

Chapter 2

Our living arrangements are very unusual, and all-the-more precious to us because of it. The house comes with the position of caretaker at the *Piece Hall,* which was built as a venue for cloth trading in 1779. The listed building act, which came into force after the war, means they will never be able to change the house to use it for anything else.

So, it seems that while ever my father has the job of caretaker, we can live here. The history of the house and the unique way we live have seeped into our hearts over the years and become part of us. I have never known anything else.

When I'm not at work, I can be found here, in our little secret garden. It's not the same as the one Frances Hodgson Burnett describes in her wonderful book, but it was inspired by her imaginings, according to my mother. It's my second favourite place to while away the hours.

We're tucked snugly between the smoking chimneys of industrial Halifax and *Frobisher's* factory at Cragside. We nestle at the foot of the rocky shelf that juts out into the smoggy sky, overlooking our house.

When I open and close the curtains each day, I look out at the scene, and every time I enjoy a different view. In wet weather, the crags glisten with cascading rivulets of water; in summer, shadows cast by clouds fly across their face like blackbirds; when it's windy, air rushes down the face of the crag and across the town, the narrow terrace streets acting like wind tunnels. You have to brace yourself or risk being blown off your feet.

I've written poetry about that view, and never tire of gazing out of the window. I live in my own mind too much sometimes, my mother says, but I just can't seem to help it.

Today is fresh with the chill of early autumn, which means I must wear a woollen coat and hat for the first time this season. I came here with my notebook in hand to write a few lines before tea, inspired by the change from late summer to autumn, when the air is thicker, and the smell of the coal fire of home is enticing me as I leave work.

A groaning hinge startles me from my daydream. My heart races, and I almost drop my notebook onto the damp ground when I realise the second gate is opening. Nobody has ever opened that gate to my knowledge, and I assumed it was locked, though I've never bothered to try it. A strange voice invades the silence. I only sit in the secret garden with my family or with Edyth and it certainly isn't any of them speaking to me.

"Miss Foxcroft!" Elliott Frobisher exclaims. "Why, I had no idea this place even existed."

His hat is quickly in his hand, his smart overcoat tucked with a silk scarf which doesn't appear anywhere near warm enough. At the factory I'm referred to as Bridie, but on my home ground he is being courteous. I struggle for the right words, staring at him with eyes wide like a startled deer.

"I'm so sorry to disturb you, but I came across the gate quite by chance and couldn't resist taking a peep through it. How delightful it is here."

12

"Mr Frobisher, sir," I say, bouncing up from the bench. "Forgive me for being a little flustered, I wasn't expecting company this afternoon."

His smile is slight, but it softens his face, making him seem a different person to the rather aloof-looking businessman I see on the odd occasion as he strides around the factory floor. His office sits between his father's and the small clerk's office at the very top of the factory building. They live in their world, and we live in ours, so to see him in my garden is disconcerting. As though the king has come to tea.

His gaze roams the small courtyard, taking in the leggy, fading flowers in boxes, and the bench seats Archie helped our father to make when he was a boy. Once the area was a workshop, but the roof had fallen into such disrepair we removed it and retained the walls. It's a suntrap in the summertime, and we often sit here to enjoy the sunshine. 'Our little piece of heaven' is what we call it, and we stay outside chatting until all hours in candlelight, when the weather is too stifling to sleep well. Nobody can hear us, so it's as though we may as well live on the remote moorland beyond the crags. The softness of the flowers is in stark contrast to the giant stone factories swamping three of the four sides. I can only see the rooftops, making it a very private world ... or so I thought.

The secret garden is no more, I realise, now that he's discovered it tucked away at the back of our home.

"My, what a wonderful space you've created here, I'm really quite envious," he says, his face like a small boy at a fairground.

I forget it really would be a sight for sore eyes to happen across for the first time, as I'm so used to seeing it.

"Please, do sit down," I find myself saying through force of habit.

He has no hesitation, pulling the tails of his overcoat to sit on the bench against the opposite wall, his smile widening. He doesn't bother to wipe the seat first with his handkerchief, so the dampness will be soaking through the expensive wool of his coat.

I can't help feeling as though he has intruded on hallowed ground, spoiling it just by his presence. It's wrong of me to think such a thing, when, by rights, the land belongs to him and his father.

"It's a very dear place to us," I tell him. "The flower boxes were filled with fruits and vegetables during the war, but now the garden can be pretty rather than functional again. I'm surprised you haven't spotted the gate before."

"There have always been boxes and paraphernalia piled up in front of the gate since before our time. The space is positively charming. It has made my day to come across it."

My face spreads into a grin, and we lock eyes until I look down at my notebook. I've never spoken to Elliott Frobisher before in my year of working at the factory, as there was never any need. Mr Jarvis, the supervisor, oversees the factory workers, keeping a watchful eye on day-to-day matters. He has a very different approach to Alice and her name lives on when someone says, "Alice wouldn't do such-and-such," at least once a day.

It's now my turn to speak, and I bite my bottom lip, trying to think of something to say.

"What we love most about this garden is that every evening and weekend, when the workers have left to go home, the whole area feels as though it belongs to us," I say.

"I can imagine, as it's a very unusual living situation you have here. Very exclusive, one might say."

Exclusive makes me think of a rambling house with a garden that has no end in sight, so you wonder what treasures lie beyond. I would never describe our humble home in such a way.

I hope he might make his excuses soon and return to his day. It must surely be home time for him, though he and his father work longer hours than us.

Clearing his throat, he looks down at the twiggy red begonias. The flowers last longer in the season due to the sheltered spot and we pour used tea leaves from the teapot over them, which they seem to like.

"At Christmastime we have the area to ourselves for two whole weeks when the businesses close, and we're often snowed in. Archie and I used to sledge down the empty cobbled streets on old tin trays," I gabble. "Our favourite place to sledge back then was on the far side of the crag, where stones give way to the moorland sedge. It's more of a hill, but very steep, and it made us go so fast."

I'm telling him too much when he has no interest in my childhood memories. Even so, he seems to be listening attentively from politeness, no doubt.

"So, how are you finding your position at the factory?" he asks. "I have never had the opportunity to ask before."

I'm nothing more than the daughter of the caretaker to him, so I've no idea why he feels he must stay and make small talk with me. Thankfully, this is an easy question to answer.

"Oh, I love working there, thank you, sir. I always wanted a job at *Frobisher's*, and I was very happy when Edyth said there was a vacancy. They're few and far between, as you know, so I've been lucky."

His lips are pursed as he listens, but his eyes are still twinkling with the hint of a smile. He has gentle eyes, as my mother would say, and they appear almost friendly, as though we're far more acquainted than exchanging a moment or two of conversation.

I've been at the factory for over a year already and I've loved my time there as much as I hoped I would. Working so close to home and alongside Edyth has made me feel as though I've been living in a little dream; the world of a child, playing dolls with my friend and being paid for the pleasure. I have been contented all year.

"I'm very pleased to hear it. Your father has been a loyal employee for nearly twenty years, so I imagine you will have been the first choice for Mr Jarvis when your name was mentioned." He pushes up the collar of his coat from the creeping cold. "I understand you and Miss Appleyard are firm friends."

"Yes, she visits most days as she's from a large family, so it's a little quieter here … as you might imagine," I add.

He laughs, tipping his head back briefly, so he looks almost boyish. As I watch him, I suddenly recall how Edyth told me he was married, but his wife seemed to disappear into thin air not long after he came back from the war. The whispers flew around the factory about her being locked up or even murdered; these rumours tend to get out of hand quickly. Mr Jarvis often warns us about tittle-tattling, but it's just part of life in Halifax and no doubt any close-knit town. I might ask my father if he knows anything more about her whereabouts.

"You have indeed created a little haven here, Miss Foxcroft. I would lose many an hour sitting here alone if it was mine. Sometimes, I long for a little privacy myself, somewhere I could retreat to that nobody else knows about. What a luxury."

I doubt there are many luxuries he and his father are missing in life, though I suppose privacy is something that can't be bought.

His face is half in shadow by now as twilight is descending. The nights are drawing in and my mother will be coming to fetch me inside for tea. What a shock it would be for her to see our visitor sitting on a bench chatting away to me.

"I hear Miss Appleyard is walking out with your brother and has been for quite some time. Perhaps wedding bells might be on the horizon before too long," he says.

The turn in conversation seems too personal to discuss with him, especially as it isn't about me. My father must keep him informed of family matters for him to know so much.

"I think I would be the first to know from Edyth and the last to know from Archie if they ever decided to tie the knot," I say lightly.

My eyes drift to our gate, and he follows the trail.

"I'm sorry, I must let you go inside," he says, seeming to read my mind. "I hope you will forgive my impromptu visit, Miss Foxcroft. I shall leave you to your evening."

His gaze finds mine, but for too long, setting my cheeks on fire. I can barely look his way as I sit frozen to the spot. If he doesn't tear his eyes away from my face soon, I will have to find the strength to make my excuses and leave.

His bold conduct is making my heart pound, and I'm giving him approval by tolerating such behaviour, as my father would say.

"All that remains for evil to triumph is that good men do nothing," he's been known to quote, or something along those lines. I agree, except I can't imagine that Elliott Frobisher is an evil man.

I wonder now how I can put an end to the conversation without appearing rude to my employer.

"Come again anytime," I say with a blurt, and I'm as shocked as he is by the invitation.

It takes him a moment to respond, and then he only says, "I shall, thank you, Miss Foxcroft. I've enjoyed our little chat very much this evening."

He bows his head before disappearing through the gate in his black coat like a magician in a stage act, only needing to be followed by a puff of smoke.

I curse myself for allowing nerves to take control of my mouth. His face may have been in shadow, but there was no mistaking how it lit up at my unexpected invitation. I can only hope now he doesn't think I'm leading him up the garden path.

I pick up my notebook with a sigh that rings around the walls, and stare at the rusty bolt on the gate. I wonder now if I should try to slide it back into its bed.

For this path I have unwillingly paved for him through sheer panic, can surely only lead the both of us to nowhere.

Chapter 3

Come what may, when the whistle blows at the factory, everything stops for tea at eleven o'clock sharp. Whatever is going on in the world outside those four walls, it's of no concern to us as we down tools, departing in a twisting snake of a queue to troop downstairs to the canteen for a strong cup of tea and a biscuit. I, for one, look forward to the simple pleasure of it every weekday morning.

Seventy-four doll makers—potters, painters, dressers, and packers—all come together to create a deafening clamour that rings around the wooden floors and brick walls of the canteen. Mr Jarvis will not tolerate any talking whatsoever on the shop floor, and we're not fool enough to disobey him, so there's always plenty to discuss.

We all mingle at the long tables with bench seats, but there's a definite pecking order among the workers. The artists are the most skilled workers, and they seem to know it, keeping to themselves at break times. The potmen, as we call them, are a decent crowd, not too high and mighty, even though I marvel at how they can craft such delicate and lifelike faces from the clay.

Edyth and I are dressers. We add hair and clothes to the painted porcelain dolls before the packers carefully place them in their boxes, ready for their new homes.

I was terrified of dropping the bodies when I first started. You get docked a shilling if you break one, but Edyth gave me a tip about rubbing my hands with witch hazel before we start work to keep them dry. We keep a bottle handy under the worktable.

The two of us always end up chatting together. It somehow seems to happen naturally after a minute or two of banter with our colleagues. They call us *Snow White and Rose Red,* like the characters from the fairytale, as Edyth is as fair as I am dark.

We wear the same uniform of black cotton dresses with a white collar and cuffs, and our hair is worn in the popular chin-length waves. I must admit, we make a good pairing despite our differences.

"Well, Bridie, you'll never believe it, but your brother and I are going to see the new Bette Davis film tomorrow night," she tells me, tucking her hair behind her ear, a little smile lifting her lips.

I almost splutter my tea. "You mean to tell me our Archie is going to watch a romantic film? I never thought I'd see the day, Edyth. He must be smitten, is all I can say."

She shrugs, her eyes creasing, and I'm reminded how pretty she is with her high cheekbones and small features. These are but a few of the reasons my brother is so taken with her.

"He says he doesn't mind, and it's supposed to be good, so there we have it. He's a changed man, I tell you."

Oh, how I hope she's right, though to be fair, a year is the longest my brother has ever walked out with anyone. When he has a drink or two in him, he becomes sentimental, admitting to being in love, but he'd never forgive me if I mentioned it the next day. Edyth told me he's said the words to her, brushing over the details as she's talking about my brother, and I'm thankful for her sensitivity.

"We just need to find somebody for you, Bridie," she says, patting my arm now.

I heave a silent sigh because this little comment is what I hear often from Edyth and my mother, but there's nobody who interests me. The men at the factory are either spoken for or simply not to my liking in that way. I'd be a fool to jump at the first person who asks me out because, the way I see it, the rest of my life is one heck of a long time.

"I'm happy at home with my mam and da, and my brother ... for the most part."

I roll my eyes, making her laugh. "Oh, you love each other really," she says. "Anyway, I thought I would take the opportunity to mention something I've been waiting to share. I just happen to know Sid Parker in despatch has his eye on you and he has for quite some time."

She glances in Sid's direction, and I swivel my head to look at him without thinking. He's watching us as his friend is chattering away, oblivious, and I turn swiftly back to Edyth, who now has a huge grin splitting her face.

"He told me last weekend when I saw him at the grocers. In fact, he was waiting outside to waylay me, hopping from one foot to the other, poor lad. I said I'd mention it to you, but of course I didn't make any promises." She leans toward me. "You know, you could do worse for yourself, Bridie."

"Well, that's a fine accolade if ever there was one," I say. "I'm sorry, but that's not enough to tempt me. Sid's nice enough as far as I can tell, but I don't see myself with him."

Finishing my tea, I munch on a custard cream, mulling over her confession. I always save the best until last to savour it.

"You'll be left on the shelf with that attitude, miss. How can you know if you're a match unless you go out with him?"

"So, you're with my brother so you're not left on the shelf then. Wait until I tell Archie, he will be heartbroken," I say.

She nudges me with her shoulder.

"That's not true, I'm head over heels, though you better not tell him. No, the point is, there's limited opportunity for all of us and it's the luck of the draw if you happen to meet someone special. Look at Archie and me, it took years to discover how we feel about each other."

Perhaps she's right. I might be being picky, but surely there must be some kind of spark or attraction to begin with. Edyth looks at me over her teacup, one eyebrow tilted.

"Oh, alright then, I'll think about it," I say as the whistle goes to signal break time is over. She nods her approval. There's a scraping of chairs and a clatter of boots on floorboards as everybody scrabbles to their feet to return to the shop floor. Mr Jarvis will give us one of his terrifying looks if we dawdle on our way back; they're enough to keep all of us in line.

I can feel Sid Parker's eyes burning a hole in my dress as I walk past his table and sneak a little glance in his direction. He smiles and I do the same before taking Edyth's arm. That wasn't so terrible.

As I sit at the worktable ready to pick up where I left off with the doll I abandoned for tea, I spot the back of Elliott Frobisher's dark head of waves as he strides towards the lift to go up to his office.

Sid springs to mind as a nice, straightforward, boy-from-next-door type of character, not the wealthy owner of a factory, who just so happens to be my employer.

The lift door closes, but not before he gives me a hint of a smile and the slightest incline of his head. My suspicions are confirmed; I *did* give the wrong impression yesterday, and so a game of cat and mouse begins.

I swing my eyes left to check if Edyth saw what just took place, but she and the rest of the table are busy working—as I should be.

The half-assembled doll sits in my hands, and I resume my task with forced vigour, trying to sweep the man clean from my thoughts.

My busy hands begin to tremble as I realise that I never mentioned our strange encounter to Edyth, though I had ample opportunity to tell her at break time.

So, now I have a secret.

This will never do because if I know anything at all, it's that secrets bring a person nothing but trouble.

Chapter 4

I wait all week for Sunday afternoons. Each time I glance up from our front window, I think of Sundays, when I wander up to the top of the crags to look down upon our house. I enjoy the wonderful view stretching for miles up there, and over the years it's become a moment of peace I look forward to.

We always breakfast on porridge, bacon and eggs then have a hearty Sunday dinner of roast beef and Yorkshire puddings, so I'm ready to walk it all off by the time three o'clock chimes on the town hall clock.

"Be careful up there today, Bridie, it looks like it might snow," my mother calls from her fireside chair as I'm buttoning my coat. "Make sure you wear your long boots just in case you get caught out."

I open the front door to see the heavy sky and do as my mother asks, layering my scarf and popping on my woollen mittens to keep the chill at bay. The crags are calling me, and how disappointed I would be to miss a week just because of a peppering of snow.

The cobbled street in front of our house slopes downhill before I cross the road at the bottom to begin the steep climb. It quickly takes my breath, but I remind myself it's worth the discomfort once I'm at the top. Despite the wild wind up here, moss and ancient bushes still somehow manage to cling on for dear life to the side of the rock. The tiny stone cottages become sparser the higher I climb, and the crags feel more as though they belong to me. It takes a good fifteen minutes to make it to the summit as I think of it, and when I finally stand looking down upon our house, the snow begins to flurry. My mother was right.

The breathtaking view of the town with my home, and the *Piece Hall* nestled in front, greets me through the snowflakes. I picture my mother sewing in the parlour and my father having a snooze after coming home from the lunchtime session at the pub and indulging in a roast dinner. Archie will be getting ready to go to Edyth's house for tea with her mother and six siblings. It must be love, I think, as he's never gone home to a girl's house before, at least as far as I know.

Movement in the corner of my eye startles me, and I whip my head to see Henry Friar opening the gate to a cottage. It's not his own cottage, the one he shares with his grandmother since his parents and grandfather died, it's Mrs Calder's, who lives alone. He will have approached up the hill from the other direction, but I've never come face to face with him since the war.

Under the circumstances, I'm not sure how I should react.

I rarely hear mention of Henry's name nowadays, but once he was the talk of the town. That's not to say he's been forgotten, not by a long chalk. He never went to fight because he has a small farm and, as a result, was exempt from conscription.

"Two carrots and a sprout surely can't be classed as farm," I've heard my father say. "He should have paid his dues like the rest of the lads." His face clouded when he spoke of him; an expression I see whenever Henry's name escapes someone's lips.

Henry was one of only three men from the town who didn't go to fight. The other two have moved away since, unable to face the humiliation. Henry's name has been muddied around these parts ever since, and he shall not be allowed to forget it.

"Hello, Bridie," he says, removing his cap, his mouth tight and unsmiling.

I glance around to see if anyone is looking, already knowing the answer. I never usually see another living soul up here.

"Hello, Henry," I say. There's a second or two of awkward silence which somehow, I must fill; it appears I have a nasty habit of it. "I can't believe I haven't bumped into you before now."

A redness creeps from his neck to his forehead, and I'm almost sorry for him despite my good intentions. I imagine he barely speaks to anyone, or that anyone speaks to him these days, making me wonder why he's never moved away like the others. Surely life would be easier for him if he were living anonymously in another town.

"I've been calling to give Mrs Calder a hand since she had a fall. She's a good pal of my gran's and as you know, she doesn't have any family to look after her," he says.

I wasn't expecting that, and I wonder if the townspeople would care to know as much. Regardless, I doubt it would make any difference as their resentment runs deeper and murkier than the bed of the sea.

Henry is nearer to Archie in age, and they were good friends, along with the other boys in their gang, before they went to war. He gives me a shy smile, his hand on the gate, ready to leave. My heart drops, and for some reason it's important to me to brighten his day in some small way.

"How's your gran?" I ask.

He drops his hand, his brows lifting at the straightforward question.

"Oh, you know, it's been hard for her since grandpa died." He pauses, perhaps deciding whether to go on. "We have each other, though, and that's more than some can say."

There isn't a hint of bitterness in his words, only frank honesty. It's suddenly not only the snowflakes that are stinging my eyes as I stare at him. Henry was always polite, never in any trouble at school, and now he's been made a recluse up here. I've never seen him in town, but surely, he must need to go for provisions—I imagine the poor man dreads it from one trip to the next.

"I wonder if it might have been better for you both to move, Henry," I say, brushing my eyes with my mittened hand. Regret comes quickly when I realise the statement only highlights his difficult circumstances, setting his face alight again.

"I wish I could, Bridie, believe me, and we've spoken about it, but I think it would finish gran if we left the … farm. She's never lived anywhere else, so it wouldn't be right. I couldn't do it to her." His voice is slightly high, as though I've touched a raw nerve, and I have.

So, this explains why they must live this reclusive life of misery. Nobody in their right mind would be made a prisoner in their own home if they had an alternative.

What happened to his parents, I wonder. I've never heard anyone speak of them, even in rumour, unlike Mrs Frobisher, and he's only ever lived with his grandparents since I've known him. He's been around all my life, yet he's still a stranger.

He glances up at the charcoal clouds, the snowflakes thickening, as we stand here in silence.

"You'd better be thinking about getting home before the snow starts to settle. I've seen you up here before, Bridie, but you know …"

The next unspoken words hang in the air, settling around us so I think the tears might escape. I grapple for a gulp of cold air, snowflakes settling on my tongue.

"If you see me again, be sure to say hello, Henry. Three o'clock most Sundays, weather permitting."

His smile makes me feel as though I've handed him a gift. I might enjoy the pleasure of it, but my thoughts now return to the consequences of being seen talking to the most hated man in town.

He nods, his smile lingering, before replacing his cap and disappearing down Mrs Calder's path. I imagine him washing her pots and checking she has everything she needs, before heading back home to have a dreary Sunday evening with his grandmother. This is no life for a young man; he should be earning a decent crust at the mill, then drinking with his pals afterwards at the *Feathers*.

The snow is whitewashing my coat as I peer down through the bushes and past the drop of the crags to the town below. Our brief encounter has unsettled me.

Our house is only a few hundred yards away as the crow flies from where I stand, the gentle glow of the parlour lamp calling me home as much as the crags called me here.

For a long time, nothing of significance happened in my life and now, in the space of three weeks, I've had two very strange encounters.

Yet neither would sit well with my family, and for entirely different reasons. Sid Parker is becoming a more appealing alternative by the day.

Chapter 5

Mother and I gather around Edyth like a pair of clucking hens. She extends her hand, and we wait to coo in turn at her new engagement ring.

"Well, I never! I don't think I've set eyes on a more beautiful ring," my mother says, turning Edyth's hand so it sparkles in the light.

"I know, Annie, your son has very good taste, it must be said," Edyth says, smiling over the top of my head at Archie.

My brother is beaming like sunshine on a winter's day as I pull him into my arms for what I expect to be a clumsy embrace. For once though he doesn't pull away immediately, he keeps his hand on my back, and I sink into the newness of the feeling. This Christmas Day is one for a little sentimentality if ever there was one. His warm embrace tells me he's of the same mind.

"So, we're officially to become sisters," I say to Edyth, running my thumb over the single diamond of her ring. It twinkles my way, almost as a symbol of the happiness to come in our entwined futures.

"You've always been like a second daughter, Edyth. I've always said as much, haven't I, Bridie?" my mother says, catching a tear with her handkerchief.

This is the Christmas I will remember above all others, I think. The year ahead beckons with the joy of a wedding and then, who knows, this time next year we might be awaiting the arrival of a new addition to the family. Now, that would just be the icing on the cake.

The room is filled to the brim with festive spirit as we sit down to dinner. We decorated the tree in early December and made sure we had plenty of coal that will last us through the harshest winter months. The early part of the year ahead will no doubt be spent planning the wedding, which they hope to be in July, they tell us. My mother and I must start sewing a new quilt if it's going to be ready in the midst of the busy preparations.

It's decided that the newlyweds will live with us after they marry until they can find a place to rent in town. A cloud hovers when I think ahead to the day when Archie will no longer be living here, though it was always going to happen one day. I'm only thankful I'll see Edyth at the factory every day at least.

"A son is a son until he finds a wife, a daughter is a daughter for the rest of her life," my mother has quoted over the years, always with a rueful look in her eye. I wonder if she's thinking of it today. If she is, Edyth, if anyone, will make sure my brother is the exception to the rule.

After dinner, Edyth and Archie leave us to spend the rest of Christmas Day with Edyth's lively brood. Once I might have called myself, but today is for the future bride and groom to share their special news.

My mother tells me it will be a relief to sit down and put her feet up after the busy morning we've had. She's keen to make a start on her new book, and my father settles down with a tot of whisky. The radio is humming low with Christmas carols in the background as I head up to my room.

Through the condensation of the window, the secret garden is waiting. I think of it now as the perfect place to sit and perhaps do a little sewing for my new project if I wrap up warmly. Life will become busy once the New Year is upon us, and I may not have a chance to indulge in some time to myself there for quite a while.

The scene is prettied by the snow which has been kind until now, only lightly dusting the landscape. Soon it will be knee deep and my walks to the top of the crags will be curtailed for a while. I pull my festive red cardigan tighter around me.

I've seen Henry eight Sundays in a row since our first meeting. I know he waits for me, and I don't mind the thought of it, only I'm careful to make sure we're alone still. This has begun to shame me when he's nothing but kind. I too would seek company if I lived as lonely a life as he.

He doesn't buy provisions in the town as I thought, which is why I've never bumped into him over the years. He grows fruit and vegetables himself as he always has, but now he walks in the other direction to a village shop six miles away where they buy his surplus stock. This allows him to buy meat, cheese, and other sundries, and he and his grandmother live frugally. They pay their rent from the eggs the hens produce, and Henry doing odd jobs for people round and about. It's just far enough away for them not to put two and two together, and I hope it stays that way for both their sakes.

His Christmas Day will be very different to ours, and the thought of it pains me now.

I swing from the window, grabbing the misfit doll I'd asked to bring home from work, and my bag of rags. Adding an extra cardigan, I head downstairs to find my warmest coat and boots from the closet. I catch my mother's distant look in her eye as she glances up from her book, her head still partly in her make-believe world. She only smiles but makes no comment because she knows where I will be heading. My father is dozing by the fire, and I soak up the cosy Christmas scene before I leave them behind, closing the door quietly on my way out.

Our small yard has been spruced for Christmas, along with the rest of the house, and I take the rusted giant key from the hook by the gate to unlock it. Peace hits me like a gentle breeze as soon as I step into the garden, and I sweep the snow from the bench with my hand. The area is made silent by Christmas, and I bask in it a moment after all the hurly-burly earlier. The day has been filled with joy, yet somehow my thoughts are not quite settling on the good news as they should be.

The now familiar creak of the second gate opening makes my head fly in its direction, heart pounding. I've been wondering when, rather than if, I might receive another visit from Elliott Frobisher for weeks now. I imagined, of all the days I would be safe, it would be Christmas Day. But here he is, standing in front of me with ruddy cheeks and a hesitant smile.

"I took a gamble. I thought I might find you here today, Miss Foxcroft," he says. Taking off his hat, he flicks his starched handkerchief over the snowy bench opposite. "I hoped it was as good a time as any to accept the kind invitation you extended. Merry Christmas to you."

I somehow manage to swallow the shock of his reappearance to wish him the same. "I hope you've had a pleasant day so far," I add quickly.

He shrugs and shakes his head. "Frankly, it's been rather dull, and I was ready to take a walk in the fresh air, whether I won my gamble or not. I trust the day has been somewhat livelier in your household."

He's wearing a different style of coat, more like the one my father wears to church only of a better quality. It makes him look younger and somehow more 'one of us' which is a favourite saying of Archie's. He can look rather austere walking around the factory. That is until he manages to catch my eye at an opportune moment. This little ritual has gone on for some weeks now, and it's not something I look forward to.

"Lively is an apt description. You were right, wedding bells are in the air. My brother has announced he is to marry Edyth, Miss Appleyard, and we could not be happier."

His teeth flash my way, white as the snow at our feet, and I can't help but return his genuine smile.

"Indeed, this is such good news, I must congratulate your father when we return to work in January. You especially will be happy to welcome her into the family, I'm sure."

"Yes, it's true, Edyth and I have lived in each other's pockets since we were children. Archie is lucky to have her." I consider the statement further, feeling disloyal as he watches me. "There again, my brother will look after her well, because we've had a decent upbringing."

His gaze is steady, holding my face.

"You and your brother have certainly come from good stock. I have never heard a bad word said about your father in all the years he's worked for us."

My cheeks burning, I look down at the half-dressed doll on my lap.

"I wonder ..." his words trail away. "No, I'll give it some more thought, but I'd like to help the celebrations along in some way if I can, and I'm sure my father will feel the same."

He makes no mention of it, but the silence that falls around us forces me to feel the need to hide the doll in my ragbag.

"It was going to be thrown away with the rest of the misfits, the glaze hadn't taken properly on the body," I tell him. "I asked Mr Jarvis if I could bring her ... it home."

His palm flies in the air, saying quickly now, "Of course, please don't alarm yourself. I'm only curious what you plan to do with the doll, is all."

I hold the doll in front of me, feeling very foolish as I study my work in progress. It was just an idea I had for Edyth, and it was only meant to be between the two of us.

"Well, it's silly really, but like you I thought my brother might propose before too long, so I've been planning ahead," I say, raking my fingers through the doll's dark hair as I wonder how on earth to explain. "It's just that Edyth loves Princess Elizabeth as we all do, but more. She keeps cuttings from newspapers and magazines and I'm sure she prefers the newsreels more than the film when we go to the *Regal* picture house. So, I thought what better gift than making a copy of the princess's engagement outfit for this doll to wear? I have another misfit doll I plan to dress in the princess's wedding gown. I hoped they would make very unusual but also personal gifts."

I glance up to see him looking between me and the doll which seems very homemade and childish now I've spoken of my idea out loud.

"How perfectly delightful, I'm sure she will treasure the gifts. I'm aware myself how popular the young princesses have become in recent years. You really are a young lady of hidden talents, Miss Foxcroft."

The light is dulling, the icy air turning our breath to mist. I smile coyly at his compliment while still hoping he will soon make his excuses and leave. I'm so unused to being in the glow of the spotlight.

"I would welcome the chance to see the finished results if you would care to show them to me," he says.

His request is unexpected, a flicker of pride stirring my heart.

"Of course, if you'd like me to. I don't imagine it will take too long as a needle and thread are no stranger to me, they're like an extension of my right arm."

He chuckles softly at the notion as I gather my things, seeing this as an opportune moment to put an end to our meeting.

"I must go in for tea, and I'm sure your … your father will be wondering where you are," I say. I was going to say, 'your family' but that wouldn't be right when there's only the two of them living at the Frobisher house.

I still regret my choice of words when his smile slips from his face.

"It's unlikely my father will know I've even left the house," he says.

His smile returns too brightly. He looks almost ghoulish with his pinched cheeks and lips.

"One day you must pay a visit to my home so I might return the favour. Perhaps you could bring the dolls along to show me," he says.

What a bold and odd request. What can I possibly say? My mouth grows dry as I wonder if I would even like to see his home. If I did, it would be purely out of curiosity and nothing more.

"Don't you think such a visit would set tongues wagging, sir?"

He waits a moment before rising from the bench seat to extend his hand. I hesitate, but only briefly, before allowing him to pull me gently to my feet. It would be impolite to refuse such a gesture for no good reason; this applies to so many of his requests I now realise.

"Tongues will wag whatever one does, and you would do well to remember that, Miss Foxcroft. People with little lives have nothing better to do and we must rise above it."

My eyes flutter to his then away again in one swift movement like a bird fleeing from the heat of the sun. He drops my hand, and it's as though he's released me. His nearness is too intimate for comfort.

"I hope you enjoy the rest of your Christmas break," he says, dipping his head before heading to the factory gate.

He's gone before I can answer, and my heartbeat steadily slows now I know I shan't see him again for the rest of the holiday. I head back into the house with an uneasy knot in my stomach.

My mother is slicing the leg of ham for tea—another special treat—in the kitchen. My father, who's sitting with her at the table, sneaks a piece of it as she bats his hand away.

"Are you alright, love?" she asks, before I hang up my coat and return my boots to the rack. She's clearly spotted something in my expression, so when I lift my head, I make sure I have a smile fixed in place.

"Yes, I'm fine, mam. It's just dropped far too cold out there now to be sitting around."

She returns to slicing the ham as my father leans back in his seat, his mind seeming elsewhere as I pull out a chair to join them around the table.

"Oh, you've just reminded me, Bridie," he says, "I never got round to putting the boxes back that young Mr Frobisher asked me to move months ago. It was on my list to do before we broke up for the holiday." He runs his palm over his chin as his words begin to sink in. "I wonder now though if I might start using it as a shortcut to the factory. I imagine it was why they put the gate there years ago in the first place. It seems daft now not to use it."

He piles two doorstops of bread and butter on his plate whilst the knot turns into a brick thudding into the depths of my stomach. I'm not at all excited at the thought of my mother's Christmas ham tea for once.

Elliott Frobisher has been watching me; he must have known of the gate's existence all along. He's a dark horse, I sensed it, and this confirms he's not to be trusted. My instincts appear to have been right about him. Our 'chance meeting' was all a ruse, and the knowledge is making me feel quite sick as I finish setting the table.

My father's hard-earned wages for our annual treat are set to be wasted if I'm unable to pull myself together, and whatever I do, I must not let that man spoil this special day for us.

I must not give him the power, or I shall never get it back.

Chapter 6

"I've no idea why he wants to see you to be perfectly frank, Bridie, but he's asked me to escort you to his office. Come on now, don't dilly dally and keep a busy man waiting."

I can almost feel the colour draining from my face as I glance at Edyth. She has a small doll's arm and hand hanging from her fingers, the sight of it only adding to this peculiar moment.

"Go on, Bridie, you haven't done anything wrong so don't look so guilty," she says, with an encouraging smile. I return one over my shoulder, so my friend won't be worrying about me, as I follow closely on the heels of Mr Jarvis.

We silently travel the two floors in the lift until the doors open onto unknown territory, at least for me. I have never before been on the top floor, and this alone is enough to unnerve me. Even when I used to help my father with his rounds as a child, he never invited me up here, it always remained forbidden territory.

Mr Jarvis knocks on the wide door with the brass plaque stating, *Mr E Frobisher, Director*. He enters when called, gesturing with his head for me to follow.

"Ah, thank you, Jarvis," Elliott Frobisher says, placing his pen on the desk. "You may head back downstairs as I'm sure you have plenty to do."

Mr Jarvis shoots me a look that tells me he's certain now that I'm in trouble. I drop my eyes to the woollen carpet, the gesture no doubt only confirming his suspicions.

"As you wish, sir," he says, bowing slightly before heading to the door.

Mr Frobisher waits until the door closes before getting up from his desk chair.

"Please, do take a seat, Miss Foxcroft. I shan't keep you from your duties long, but I have something to discuss with you. There's nothing to concern yourself about, in fact I ask you here to discuss a rather pleasant matter."

This brings me no comfort. What pleasant matters could he possibly need to discuss with me rather than my father? I haven't been foolish enough to sit in the garden since Christmas, so this will be why I've been summoned here like an errant child to the headmaster's office.

This office is the largest room I have ever been inside. A family could live quite comfortably within these four walls, I think, as he sits back down on the other side of the desk. He looks every inch the businessman he is. I cast my mind back now to his more relaxed attire on Christmas Day in the secret garden. The memory of that day and his hidden intentions still makes my skin creep when I think of it. The thought of being watched is not a pleasant one.

"Well now, the reason I've called you upstairs today is that I've spoken to your father about the forthcoming wedding next July and offered the use of the canteen for the reception."

Oh, that wasn't what I expected. What a kind gesture on his part and after a moment or two of reflection, I can only see this as good news.

"How generous of you, and Mr Frobisher, sir. I know it will save Edyth and Archie a great deal of money, and the room is large enough to accommodate the whole town should they want to invite them."

I'm exaggerating, of course. I happen to know Edyth would prefer a smaller wedding, but everyone in the factory will expect an invitation. Then there's her enormous extended family at the top of the guest list. Edyth has been worrying about the expense, especially as her father is no longer with us. My father is breaking with tradition and footing the vast majority of the bill, but this will be a struggle for him on his wages.

"Thank you, I'm glad you approve. However, the reason I've summoned you here is to say that I think the room must be made fit for a wedding, with flowers, decorations, and such. I know little of these things, but I do know a wedding must be as pleasing on the eye as possible. I propose an allowance for food, drink and decorations. I've known your father since I was little more than a child after all, and my father is in full agreement as I suspected."

You know little of a wedding, I think, as I listen to him speak, yet you were married once. Where is your wife now; what has become of her? I shudder at the unwelcome questions when this is meant to a pleasant conversation.

"I know they would be very grateful for your kind offer, Mr Frobisher. Shall I tell Edyth when I return downstairs?" I ask.

He lifts his shoulders and smiles as though he's excited himself by the prospect.

"Please do, but I did wonder if you might keep the room decorations as a surprise for her and your brother.

I'm sure you and your mother would be able to do an excellent job between you with your creative skills."

I walked in here quaking with dread, and now I'm almost giddy for the months of planning ahead of us. The bride and groom's money worries have been swept aside after one short conversation.

He continues to stare at me, so I clear my throat.

"Will that be all, sir?" I ask, keen to leave the room and rejoin Edyth. Home time will soon be upon us, and then I'll be able to share the news.

His hands are locked under his chin, his forefingers creating a steeple to rest upon. His eyes are glazed until they meet mine.

"Have you finished the princess doll yet? I thought it a wonderful idea, and if you have I should very much like to see it."

All too soon my heart begins to race again, and I slide a hand down my hair. He seems insistent on pursuing this. The homespun outfits for the dolls were just a little idea for a gift, so I never expected them to be such an important topic of conversation.

Edyth's eyes lit up like the moon when I gave her the engagement doll on New Year's Eve. She told me she'd never received a more thoughtful gift, and I knew she wasn't soft-soaping me, as she would call it. Her family is so large, she often has hand-me-down clothes and gifts.

"I'm afraid it's had to take a back seat as my mother and I have been busy making the quilt for their wedding day. I hope to get back to the doll once we've finished."

His disappointment is clear, by both the drop of his small smile and his hands to his lap.

"Ah, I see. Yes, of course, the quilt most certainly takes precedence. I can't wait to see the dolls when they're finished as I imagine they will be rather lovely." He pauses, taking up his pen, and I wait to be dismissed. "Well, I must let you return to your duties before Mr Jarvis becomes agitated with us. Good day to you, Miss Foxcroft."

"Good day, sir," I say, thankful to head to the lift to return to the bustling factory floor. It beckons me as a place of safety, though there should have been nothing to fear from this conversation.

I press the lift button and tug the white collar of my uniform dress as I wait, hoping I won't be struck down for the lie I've just told.

Both dolls were completed over the Christmas break. My mother found an old copy of *Picture Post* for me to work from and I'm really pleased with the quality of the dress and the attention to detail. The bridal doll now sits waiting under the bed in a wooden box my father made me, ready to give to Edyth on the big day.

There was not a chance on this earth of me telling Elliott Frobisher as much. The man may be handsome, but his manner is off-putting. My mother often says that, if nothing else in life, we must trust our instincts to guide us.

I'm beginning to understand now that wolves can hide perfectly well in sheep's clothing.

Chapter 7

Finally, and not before time, the snow has melted enough to allow me to take my walk up the side of the crag. It's been weeks since I was able to indulge in my Sunday afternoon pleasure. How I've missed it, finding myself restless and unable to concentrate throughout the never-ending day. Sundays can make me feel like a caged lion.

Edyth's upcoming marriage to my brother has become something of a double-edged sword, as it's slowly dawned on me that I see less of her now. Preparations for the wedding are going full steam ahead with the bunting, decorations and the quilt almost finished.

My contentment at *Frobisher's* has disappeared; I'm pensive, constantly on guard and looking over my shoulder. Elliott Frobisher hasn't summoned me to his office again but still I wait for his command. I avoid the secret garden for the same reason and the safe, snug environment where I once lived and worked now gives me no peace.

An exhilarating sense of freedom mounts with each step up the crag side and I bask in it. Soon spring will be here, but for now the biting cold is still with us.

Approaching my favourite place, I spot something new. A wooden bench has appeared, and Henry's face is in profile as he sits, staring down at what I consider my very own special view. Somehow though it doesn't feel as though he's intruding on it.

I'm only a few footsteps away when he turns his face towards me, his smile so endearing that I realise I've missed him far more than the view. The thought makes my heart pound in my ears as I watch him, the clouds and endless sky framing his upper body. He has been in my thoughts too many times of late.

For once I don't check to see if we're alone, I only slide onto the new wooden seat beside him as our eyes meld. My throat is tight; I can't speak or even return his smile as I sit only inches away from his side.

"You made this for me?" I whisper eventually, still sitting in his eyes.

He turns his face back to the view through the gap in the hedge.

"I had a few bits of old wood that I thought I'd put to good use."

I run my hand over the coldness of the bench seat, the perfect smoothness of the wood sliding under my palm like a swathe of silk.

"It's beautiful, Henry," I say, my voice breaking. "How will I ever be able to thank you enough for such a gesture of kindness?"

He shrugs, batting the compliment away.

"It really wasn't any trouble, Bridie, I happen to have plenty of time on my hands."

That he does, too much time, but he needn't devote it to me. I picture him in his shed in the snow making this bench with me in mind, sawing, sanding, waxing, all with the one purpose of making me happy. It tells me that we've both lived in each other's minds these last weeks.

"How have you been?" he asks as we stare down the void together at my home. Ours is the only light we see in the gloom of the winter twilight swamping the house.

I wonder how to answer the simple question. Would it be better to hide the truth? I soon think better of it.

"I've had a strange time of it if I'm being honest," I say.

Henry is not a man to lie to, he doesn't play games like Elliott Frobisher.

The floodgates fly open and it's so easy in the end to tell him of the unsettling time I've lived through since Christmas. I explain how I've felt hounded, but in such a subtle way I've wondered sometimes if I was being overdramatic or seeing things that weren't there. The words tumble from me while he listens in silence.

My gaze roams from time to time towards him, as he sits in his worn woollen coat and knitted scarf, his reddish-brown hair curling from underneath his cap. I feel as though he's catching the words as they pour out; words I've hidden inside for so long. I've had nobody to speak to about the situation, and it was weighing heavily.

"Mr Frobisher has been on the shop floor more than usual," I tell him. "But I'm mindful to keep my eyes on the worktable until the lift doors close now, so I don't succumb to his little game."

He's in no rush to answer, continuing to stare straight ahead as he mulls over my predicament.

"Perhaps he will tire of the chase," he says. "Some men are driven by it I think, but in this case its worse because of the power he has over you and your whole family. It's not acceptable."

"Precisely," I say, "and I'm fearful and resentful of his behaviour in equal measure because of it."

He turns to look at me, moving his lips in such a way I know he has words sitting on the tip of his tongue.

"After the war, he woke up one morning to find his wife gone, you know," he says flatly. "Mrs Calder told my gran. She's friendly with somebody who works at the house and there was talk of her fleeing to America."

Ah, so, his wife ran away, and to the ends of the earth by the sound of it. I shake my head at the revelation and shuffle to sit on my mittened hands.

"America. What would there be in America for her, it's the other side of the world?"

He chuckles softly, glancing at me before quickly dropping his eyes to the bench.

"I have no idea, but that was the rumour, and there's no smoke without fire … so they tell me."

There's an odd tinge to his voice. I know nothing of his parents, but I've heard so many rumours about Henry Friar himself; rumours about him turning mad up here or that he's a coward, and worse because he wouldn't go to fight for his country. I'd like to hear from the horse's mouth why he wouldn't step up, but it's a question I could never bring myself to ask him.

"How was your Christmas?" I ask him instead.

He looks at the sky with a sigh, casting his mind back.

"I would normally say the usual, but gran was poorly, so I was going in between our house and Mrs

Calder's all week. I barely noticed Christmas to be honest. Mrs Calder is well again, but gran still isn't herself even after all these weeks. The better weather can't come quick enough this year."

His life up here is so cut off without any support of friends or family. If he should become ill, there would be nobody to call on for help.

"It must get a little lonely up here," I say quietly.

His eyes meet mine again. This time, we stare unashamedly at each other, the stillness of a Sunday afternoon floating around us. I'm glad my hands are tucked under my skirt, or they might be inclined to reach out and take his own. Compassion for this man fills my heart and not for the first time.

"It used to be," he says.

A rush of heat goes up my back. It makes me jump to my feet so suddenly I must glance away quickly from his look of alarm.

"Mam will have tea started by now," I say. "I better get back before she sends the dogs out."

He's looking past me into the distance again. I miss the warmth of his eyes already.

The thought of leaving him for at least another week is bothering me.

"Thank you for making the bench, Henry. It's incredibly kind and thoughtful of you, and I hope you and I shall spend many a happy hour sitting on it."

He nods, his smile shy as he looks anywhere but at me.

You're not making this easy for me, Henry Friar, I think, as I set off back down the hill, the now greyish sludge of the snow soddening my boots.

After a moment I turn around to see him standing at the side of the bench with his hands in his pockets. I wave and he does the same before heading off in the opposite direction, no doubt to spend yet another quiet evening, but this time with a sick grandmother. I turn around more than once until he disappears over the hill.

For the first time, I don't want to go home, and the thought nothing short of scares me.

During tea, my mind is still with Henry as my mother chatters about the wedding cake she plans to start baking tomorrow. She hasn't noticed yet that she's almost talking to herself as my father also seems to be in a world of his own.

"Are you alright, da?" I ask him, taking his empty plate to start the washing up. "You don't seem to have much to say for yourself this evening."

When he comes home from the pub on a Sunday, he has a nap on the bed then he generally has plenty to tell us of the lives of his cronies who frequent the *Feathers*. There's always plenty of news, as the drink loosens lips; my mother calls him an old fishwife.

"The pair of you have been away with the pixies all weekend," she says now. "Why do you think I've been wittering away like there's no tomorrow?"

I do my mother an injustice to think for a moment that her eyes aren't all-seeing. My laugh is too high as I make to stand up. She puts her hand over mine and nods towards my father, so I sit back down again.

He's settled in his chair now by the fire, his grey hair still fluffy at the back from where he napped earlier. We sit in silence, waiting to discover what he has to say, the clock on the mantle ticking the day away.

"Well, last thing Friday, young Mr Frobisher asked me if I'd agree to our Bridie going up to the house to discuss the wedding preparations. He wants to know what it will cost so he can make sure she has all she needs," he says, his eyes never leaving the flames.

My mother turns to look at me, shrugging her shoulders with a slight, irritable shake of her head.

"Is that all, John? You put the fear of God in me then, silly man, you really did. I thought something terrible had happened."

She bustles to the sink with a sigh, and my father turns to look at me. We sit with our eyes locked, unsmiling.

His pallor, white as a ghost, and drawn expression are telling me that he's as troubled as I am about the request. I wonder now if he knows more about our employer than I do.

But as we listen to my mother clattering the pots in the sink, he also knows as well as I that there's not a damn thing either of us can do about it.

Chapter 8

"Now, you're sure you have a clean handkerchief?" my mother asks, as I open the front door.

"Yes, mam, don't worry," I tell her, my mouth twitching. "I'm not six any longer, in case you hadn't noticed."

She stops sweeping the linoleum, chuckling at me as she leans on the brush handle.

"You'll understand one day, Bridie. Once a mother always a mother, there's no getting away from it."

She gives me a little wave, telling me she's keen to hear all about the house after all the years of wondering what it looks like inside. She thinks it a day for excitement, whereas I feel as though it's my first day of school. Today is different however, as I won't have my mother's hand to hold on the way. I suggested she come with me, but she said the invitation was extended only to me so it would be impolite.

"I'll walk with you, Bridie," my father says, shrugging his arms into his coat. "I'll go on to the pub from there."

I hope my smile is enough to tell him how grateful I am as we say our farewells to my mother. Oh, to be joining her to sew by the fireside this Saturday afternoon instead.

My father raises his arm, bent at the elbow and I take it gladly as he throws my cloth bag over his shoulder for the half a mile walk through the town together. For too long we talk about anything other than our final destination, and my exasperation mounts when we're wasting time.

He blows out his cheeks, saying finally, "I'd like to come with you, Bridie, but as your mother pointed out, Mr Frobisher made no mention of it. He's a gentleman and there's no reason I can think of to refuse his invitation for you, but it bothers me nonetheless."

For the first time I wish I was from noble stock of days gone by, when it would have been unthinkable to be allowed out of my parents' sight without a chaperone.

He negotiates the wetness of the cobbles on the town pavement, still tall and straight-backed despite his age and hard work.

"What's bothering you, da?" I ask him. "I saw your face the other night."

"Oh, you know, it's just that he was married, but he's not anymore, and a father wonders about these things. I'm not worried exactly, it's more of a feeling, but then I have the consolation that old Mr Frobisher will be around."

We're both of the same mind it seems, and that thought is also some comfort to me, at least.

"Do you know anything at all about his wife?" I ask.

I keep my eyes on the cobbles but sense him glance my way.

"Not much, as she wasn't around long. Many were marrying in haste in wartime, thinking there might be no tomorrow, and many will have lived to regret it, I imagine. I don't think he murdered her though." We share a smile before his cheeks turn pink. "Can I ask though, do you like him, Bridie? I know there's plenty at the factory with their eye on him."

I pull his arm gently to come to a stop and turn to face him.

"No, I don't, da, not in that way. It's strange though, because I should be flattered by all this attention when he's so well-to-do."

We set off again, and he tells me we can't force a feeling, and we shouldn't. I'm always so thankful for the wisdom and commonsense of my parents.

Now we've broached the subject, the fresh air begins to settle me as we greet the people we know. There's plenty of them, but we delay more with some than others. Everybody knows everybody round here, yet nobody knows anybody only a few miles away.

The huge black iron gates loom all too soon and my heartbeat picks up speed. My father and I stand together admiring the grandness of the Frobisher home and the vast grounds of rhododendron and azalea that coddle the house. They're preened and well cared for, but strangely unwelcoming without their blooms. The entrance alone must have cost more to build than our entire house, with stone steps sweeping their way to the glossy black front door. Twelve twinkling windows are like six pairs of eyes watching us, watching them. I've had almost a week to reflect on this meeting; my imagination has become absurd.

The gates open when we push them, but it takes more than a small effort from my father. He gives me a smile of encouragement, as I plant a kiss on his cheek. He stands still, waiting, to watch me drag my feet up the gravel driveway.

Before I disappear, I raise my hand, expecting him to turn on his heel and head back into town, but instead he stays rooted. My sense of uneasiness about being summoned here is increasing with each step.

Someone I assume to be the butler peers from behind the door, his courteous nod telling me that I am expected.

"Good morning, I'm Miss Bridie Foxcroft and I have an appointment to see Mr Frobisher," I say.

"Please come in, Miss Foxcroft, Mr Frobisher is expecting you."

He opens the door wider, and I step into the tiled passageway which leads to the open door of the kitchen at the end.

Even the butler is a person of authority to me, but I'm surprised to see his smile is warm, putting me a little more at ease as he hangs up my coat. I certainly wasn't expecting such a hospitable welcome, as some of the butlers I've read about in my books have been fearsome. I heave a breath before I follow him, counting thirty-seven steps until he announces my arrival.

Elliott Frobisher places his newspaper on a low table before standing to greet me. His frame dominates the large room making me feel small and vulnerable already.

"Miss Foxcroft, how do you do? Denton, please would you arrange refreshments. Our guest will be no doubt need warming up after her walk."

"Very good, sir," Mr Denton says, closing the door behind him.

So, I'm alone with him now, like a little mouse come out of her house, uncertain what to do or say.

Though manners have been part of my upbringing, etiquette has a vast set of rules, and I should hate to let myself and my parents down.

I'm disappointed not to see any sign of his father, as I'd hoped.

"I must thank you for giving up your valuable time this weekend, Miss Foxcroft. Please, do take a seat," he says.

The room is homelier than the outside of the house would suggest, and looks to have been well-used over the years. I wonder if the décor was to his mother's or his wife's taste, as it has a woman's touch about it. Damask-covered settees, silk curtains and the most impressive marble fireplace; there shall be plenty to describe to my own mother when I get home.

He gestures with his hand to the opposite end of the settee where he was reading the newspaper. I make a mental note that there are two clear spaces between us as I perch on the edge of the cushion.

"I've brought the dolls for you to see, sir," I say, opening my bag. If I *must* be here, I can at least seek to keep the visit as brief as possible.

My outburst makes his eyes and lips grow round, taking a few seconds for him to respond. "How kind of you to bring them along. But there's no rush, we have plenty of time," he says, with just the hint of a smile.

I stare at the flames of the fire but they're doing nothing to warm the creeping sensation chilling my back.

"You know, there is a small coincidence in your choice of gift for Miss Appleyard," he says, crossing his long legs at the knee. "The definition of Bridie is 'princess'. Were you aware of that?"

To know such a thing would mean him having to research my name surely, and I think it rather odd he would want to go to so much trouble. The door opening makes me thankful for a brief respite from this uncomfortable meeting.

A maid appears, tea tray balanced in her hands and set beautifully with a silver stand of scones and dainty porcelain dishes of jam and cream with tiny spoons. She catches my eye on her way out, not a flicker of a smile in sight. No doubt she's had plenty to say in the kitchen about the peculiar visitor to the house this morning. Little does she know how much I should like to be her at this moment.

Matters of etiquette rear their head once more. Do I pour the tea; does he; do we eat first? I've no idea, so I wait until he pours the tea into cups pointing to the milk jug and sugar bowl. I pour the milk but leave the sugar well alone as I would no doubt make a terrible mess with my trembling hands.

"Well, now, Miss Foxcroft, I'm pleased you accepted my invitation," he says, settling back in his seat with his teacup and saucer. "I wanted to be certain you have everything in hand for the big day, but also to reimburse you for any costs you may have incurred for the room decorations."

Oh, if only I could believe this was his only intention.

"Thank you, sir, my father told me as much. However, we're happy to cover the minimal cost of materials as you are already being so generous."

I prepared this little speech when I discovered I was to come here. It would feel wrong in so many ways to take money from him, but more because I'd rather not be personally beholden to him.

"I'm a man of my word, Miss Foxcroft, I said I was happy to pay, and my offer still stands."

His eyes try to hold mine over his teacup as he takes a sip. I know he's toying with me and sadly, my nerves are making me play straight into his hands. This is all part of his ruse, as he could just as easily have discussed costs with my father.

"Well, I'll be sure to let you know in due course, sir, thank you."

I grab my bag from the side of the settee before he has a chance to say more. He wants to see the dolls and he must see them today, as I'm not giving him another excuse to invite me here again.

I pull out the first princess doll, the one with the white shorter-length dress of satin, and the tiny double string of fake pearls. I made the pearls from painted ball bearings. I pinned the doll's dark hair in exactly the same style as the princesses, finishing off the look with a little pair of shoes and a handbag made from scraps of black satin.

A quiet gasp escapes him when he sees it, and I can't help a small sense of pride. He scrambles to put down his cup and saucer to take a closer look, glancing from the doll to me then back again, his jaw hanging loosely.

"Forgive me, I'd no idea the doll's outfit would have such attention to detail," he says, running his forefinger over necklace. "I confess this was not what I was expecting, not at all."

I knew only my best work would do for Edyth, nothing that appeared homemade. I borrowed the doll yesterday on the pretence of making a coat to complete the outfit, which I intend to do now. I promised I'd take good care of her. I couldn't tell Edyth I was coming here, as then I would have needed to explain about the other meetings we had.

This man has made my life so … uncomfortable.

"May I take a look at the bride doll?" he asks me now, pulling me from my thoughts, which he would be offended to discover.

I take the doll from her wooden box, sensing his eyes on me as I peel away the layers of tissue paper. I stand her on the table, rearranging her wedding dress and veil as I do every time, almost as though I'm her bridesmaid.

His eyes have left my face to roam the intricacy of the lace, and the tiny tiara I made from costume gemstones on a headband. I think this is the better of the two, and I take the doll out from under my bed every night to look at her. It took hours of painstaking work, but I enjoyed every minute of it.

"Miss Foxcroft, I'm ashamed to say that I have misjudged you entirely," he whispers, his eyes still on the doll. "I knew the dolls would be charming gifts for your friend, but not… what I can only describe as exquisite works of art."

"Thank you, sir, I hoped to do justice to them, as they were made for two very special occasions. I want them to give Edyth a lifetime of pleasure."

"You are certainly a lady of hidden charms as well as a beautiful face," he says, his voice little more than a whisper, but loud enough.

There it is.

He holds his hand out towards me, and I shuffle further away in my seat.

I have no time though, to think how to respond, as we both must swing our faces, startled, as his father strides into the room. I stand to receive him, almost forgetting the delicate teacup and saucer in my hurry. I feel as though I've been caught in the act of stealing the family silver.

"Father!" his son exclaims, though he doesn't bother to get to his feet. "I thought you said you were playing golf this morning now the snow is clearing."

His father doesn't answer. Instead, he turns his attention to me, so the heat is rising from my chest as he stares my way.

"Good morning, Miss Foxcroft. This is a surprise. To what do we owe the pleasure of your company this morning? This is not the weather for a young woman to be out and about."

His son sits forward, busying himself with placing my doll back in her box and avoiding making eye contact with either of us.

"I asked Miss Foxcroft here this morning to discuss the wedding arrangements, and she has kindly shown me her sewing skills in the form of two delightful gifts she made for her friend, and future sister-in-law."

Mr Frobisher looks between us. Perhaps my face is showing too much distress or shame, perhaps he only wishes to put me at my ease, but he takes a doll from the table to sit down with her on the opposite settee.

"Please, do sit down," he says, but still my heart pounds. I'm thankful to see his expression soften a little as he studies the doll.

"You are indeed a talented seamstress; your work is beautiful and very …delicate. I wish all my dressers had such talent," he says. He glances my way, and I try to relax my face enough to smile.

"We were about to have scones, father. Would you care for one?" his son asks him now.

Should his father care for one or not, I'm in no state of mind to sit and eat scones with these two men.

"I'm afraid I must be getting back home, sir," I say, nodding to them both in turn. "Please forgive me, but I promised my mother we would visit the fabric shop before it closes early as it's a Saturday."

Elliott Frobisher's cheeks are puce as his eyes float about the room. I return the dolls quickly to my bag, keen now to make a hasty retreat.

"In that case, I'll ask my driver to take you home," Mr Frobisher says, pulling the chord to summon Mr Denton.

"No … no thank you kindly, sir, that will not be necessary," I say, the volume of my voice startling me even.

Mr Denton's friendly face reappears around the door; how I could kiss it right at this moment, though he would be horrified to know it.

"Our guest is leaving, Denton. Please will you ensure Joseph drops her home in my car. The weather is far too inclement today for a young lady to be taking a long walk," he says.

His eyes rest on his son who is finally getting to his feet.

"Goodbye, Miss Foxcroft," old Mr Frobisher says now. "I do hope you enjoy the rest of your weekend."

I bid father and son farewell as I follow Mr Denton from the room, blowing out a long, silent trail of breath when the door closes behind us

At the door, Mr Denton holds my coat to slip my arms inside, treating me as he would a true lady.

"I'm happy to walk home," I tell him. "I wouldn't like to put Mr Frobisher's driver to any trouble, and I also have some errands to run in the town."

He looks as though he might insist as I'm donning my hat, but then thinks better of it.

"Well, if you're sure, Miss Foxcroft, I shall explain to Mr Frobisher on your behalf," he says opening the door for me. "A pleasure to make your acquaintance."

He is such a gentleman, I think, hurriedly twirling my scarf around my neck. I slow my pace, so it doesn't seem as though I'm fleeing the house. I have done nothing to be ashamed of this morning.

On the front driveway, I spot movement through the window from the corner of my eye, my head swivelling to take a closer look.

Old Mr Frobisher is pointing and gesticulating, his face fiery and twisted with anger, and I'm unable to turn away from the drama.

His son's eyes now drift eerily towards me, and he follows them, so both men are staring at me through the glass. His father's fury now seems directed toward me, if I didn't know better.

I turn on my heel, almost falling, and then walk as quickly as I can without breaking into a shameful run down the gravel driveway. I'm delighted when I'm back on the right side of the black iron gates. I have finally escaped this dreadful morning, and I can return home to the world where I belong.

This world is for people who play games … and I have neither the skills nor the inclination to enter into it.

Chapter 9

"I'll walk you round home," Archie says, swaying with his hands in his pockets, and grinning like a madman. He's worse the wear for drink.

Still, if a groom isn't allowed to make merry on his wedding day, then it's a poor show. It's true though, he is mad, he's madly in love with Edyth and it has been plain for all to see. I would never have imagined him being so affectionate, particularly in front of his friends.

The whole of *Frobisher's* has enjoyed a truly wonderful day, and I'm only sorry now that it's come to an end.

"I'm sure I can manage the few steps it will take me to get home, Archie. Go find Edyth, and away to your room at the *Feathers*, you'll be in no fit state otherwise.

They're spending their wedding night in the room at the pub which is usually reserved for visiting businessmen when there isn't a wedding in town. His grin widens showing his 'film star teeth' as my mother calls them. I've always been proud of my big brother, and I've overheard many a comment made about how handsome he is.

"In no fit state for what?"

I shake my head, nudging him playfully with my elbow before heading down the stairs of the factory. The bride and groom will be greeted by roses, and the new quilt on their honeymoon bed. I called yesterday to put the finishing touches to the room and make it a little more welcoming.

Today has brought some much-needed light relief for everyone, after an unsettling rumour began flying around about the financial state of *Frobisher's*. They're only whispers in the canteen at the moment, so we're all trying not to jump the gun. But it's proving more difficult by the day to ignore the little cutbacks that have appeared. Overtime has virtually gone and, last week, break time biscuits were taken off the menu, to much wittering and grumbling amongst the staff. This week we've been told that any misfit dolls which aren't up to scratch must be double-checked by Mr Jarvis before discarding. They're only small adjustments, but they all help to oil the rumour machine.

We were keen to put all that to one side today as Edyth, my mother, and I prepared ourselves for the wedding. Edyth's house was far too crowded for any peace, and it made the perfect start to the day, getting ready together at our house. I set the bride-to-be's hair in rollers first thing, and whilst it was drying, I gave her the princess bride doll to unwrap.

"Bridie, you've outdone yourself this time," she exclaimed, fluffing out the wedding dress to take a proper look. "This is surely the most precious doll a girl could own."

The pleasure was in the giving. My mother watched on with misty eyes; a little dream has come true for her today.

"It's all Bridie's own work, Edyth. I had nothing to do with it," she said beaming at me with rollers coiled in her silver hair. She wore a dab of powder, and rouge, a swipe of lipstick completing her wedding look. It reminded us just what a pretty lady she is, and my father's smile when he saw her in her new dress and hat, bought on tick, only sealed it.

Edyth and I found ourselves alone for a moment when my mother went to ensure my father looked the part. She bustled from the room, telling us he would be struggling with his stiff collar and cuffs, not to mention his choice of tie.

Edyth was sitting at my mother's dressing table fiddling with her bouquet. She glanced up at me, her smile coy, and I wondered what she was about to say.

"Just this once, I wish Archie wasn't your brother, Bridie. I must admit I'm a little nervous about tonight, but I feel awkward talking about such things with you."

I wasn't expecting the swerve in conversation, my heart sinking.

But I knew I had to seize the nettle for my friend, whether it pained me or not. If I was in Edyth's shoes, I'm sure I would be overflowing with trepidation at the thought of my wedding night. The expectation would be a burden for anyone.

"I'm no expert about the 'such things', of course, other than the odd conversation I've overheard in the canteen, but I do know that how we feel about somebody shapes how we behave. I would imagine that love guides us in some way, surely." My cheeks burned, and I was unable to look her in the eye. "Anyway, our Archie will be feeling much the same, that must be some consolation at least."

We giggled, before I bent down to look in the mirror, and add yet another layer of my new lipstick. I was only too glad for a distraction. I doubt I was much in the way of help to the blushing bride, but I gave it my best shot.

I said my farewells to Edyth before Archie when I left the wedding. She was still dancing in her stunning dress from a second-hand shop in Huddersfield, which my mother altered, so it looked as though it had been made especially for her. The full skirt to her calf swished and swayed as she walked down the aisle on her older brother, Tom's arm. Archie could not hide his love, and admiration, as he waited for her to join him.

Both young and old Mr Frobisher attended the service, cutting a dash in their expensive morning suits. As I walked down the aisle with two of Edyth's sisters, who were also bridesmaids, I made sure to keep my eyes forward. Even so, Elliott Frobisher followed my every step.

Thankfully, he's been on the shop floor far less of late, and he hasn't been foolish enough to risk summoning me to his office after the heated reprimand from his father. This means I've denied myself the pleasure of the secret garden all summer long, as *I'm* not foolish enough to fall into the trap of going there only for him to reappear. Nowadays, I make sure to keep one step ahead.

Father and son declined to attend the wedding breakfast, perhaps of a mind we would have a better time without them. It was difficult to argue the point.

The canteen was unrecognisable, bursting with flowers, the iron beams strewn with our handmade bunting. Edyth clapped her hands with joy when she saw the room, and that was the third time I shed a tear, my senses brimming with all the bittersweet build-up, and planning.

It's definitely been worth all the fretting, I think now, as I leave the factory. My parents went home two hours ago, unable to keep up with us, they said, so I'd seen them off with a kiss, and a promise not to get too tipsy.

In the quiet, my mind wanders to Henry; he would have loved today if only the circumstances were different. I often catch myself wondering what he's doing, the thoughts taking me unawares, and his face has become the last thing I see before I go to sleep. I think of him this beautiful summer's night as I step on the cobbles in front of the factory, ready for the short walk home.

Shuffling footsteps sound in the silence, as someone appears from the shadows. I take a gulp of warm air and stop in my tracks.

"Miss Foxcroft, Bridie, please don't be alarmed. I only wish to speak to you a moment, then I'll leave you alone."

My heart plummets to my satin shoes when I recognise the voice.

The few sherries I've had throughout the day are making my head spin, but a spark of indignation lights somewhere deep within me. I must be careful it doesn't take hold.

"Mr Frobisher, you startled me," I say, hearing the stern tone to my voice, but caring about it far less than I normally would. A real gentleman would never creep up on a lady and frighten the wits out of her. "Thank you once again for your generous contribution to today's festivities, but if you'll excuse me, I must get home to bed." I pick up speed, but his footsteps manage to keep up with mine.

"Please, stop just a moment," he says, tugging my arm. I try to pull it free from his grasp, but it stays firmly in place. "I apologise but ... but I'm finding your dismissive behaviour intolerable."

The nerve of this man! My behaviour has been nothing but respectful and polite, because it must be so. Worse still, he will be well aware of it.

"I'm sorry, sir, I'm not sure what you mean," I say.

His palm is too warm on my upper arm, but it holds firm.

"I think you do know what I mean," he says. "You're giving me the runaround, when I'm going out of my way to be amenable to you. You're toying with me, and I don't like it at all."

His words fan the flames, and I'm too hot and tired at this moment.

"I assure you that I have not given you the runaround, as you call it. I'm just too polite to tell you ... tell you that I'm not interested in you. You are my employer and that is all, sir." The last word comes out louder than I intended, the formality failing to hide the resentment I feel.

My free hand immediately flies to my mouth to cover it, but it's too late. I've said too much, he has picked the wrong moment and forced my hand.

"Why though; why do you not find me to your liking, am I so repulsive? I could give you a good life, yet you don't seem to care."

I try once more to free my arm, which results in a small tussle. Still, he won't let me go, and the bricks of the factory walls behind him are blurring, as my head spins.

"Sir, please, you are not repulsive, you are just not someone I see as a person I could spend my life with. I would thank you to let go of my arm, I don't wish to cause offence or hurt your feelings."

My chest heaves as he stares at me in the moonlight. He's still wearing his suit from earlier with the tie hanging slightly lower. His hair has been raked with his fingers, so he doesn't look himself. Perhaps, like Archie, he's had a drink too many to be acting in such an ungentlemanly way.

"Well, as we're speaking plainly, I put it to you that you have someone else in mind who you could spend your life with," he says flatly.

He raises one eyebrow, as I shake my head in disbelief.

"No? There's nobody you might visit, someone perhaps just up the road there?"

He gestures with his head towards the crags, and I begin to tremble under his hot palm. Tears burn my eyes as we stare at each other.

"You may well tremble, Miss Foxcroft. I suggest your parents, no, I suggest the whole town, in fact, would be appalled to learn on whom you have set your sights."

His tone, I imagine, is like a barrister in a courtroom, condemning me for my wrongdoings. One tear, quickly followed by another, roll down my cheek. Only hours ago, I was crying tears of happiness, and now he has managed to spoil the day.

He only smirks and releases my arm with a thrust as though he's discarding me. How right I was to be wary of this man. I place a hand on the factory wall to steady myself and take a moment to try to stop the world from spinning. It's clear he's been following me, it's the only way he could know about Henry.

"Well then, it seems my future is in your hands, sir. You can tell my father, and you can tell the whole town. Like everything else, when it comes to you, I have no power over it."

I back away slowly from him as I speak, and thankfully, this time he stays rooted where he is.

"But don't you see, I don't *have* to tell anyone, Bridie? It's you who holds all the cards to your own future," he says. "Perhaps you should go home and sleep on it. Think of what you would like your future to look like. It could be very bright. Why waste it on a man who doesn't deserve you? You would be setting yourself up for a miserable life with him."

The meaning behind his words is obvious, tying my stomach in a tight knot. I wipe away my tears with the back of my hand, my knees threatening to buckle if I should stop walking.

So, according to the law of Elliott Frobisher, I must decide whether to break my family's heart, and ostracise us from the town, or give myself to him, when he has shown me his true colours. The colours, I somehow sensed, were hiding all along.

A fact suddenly occurs to me, and I cling to it as my last hope.

"I feel it only right to mention at this time that I've been informed you are already a married man, Mr Frobisher."

The colour draining from his cheeks is a small comfort. He takes a few steps towards me, but stops when I back away.

"You're quite right, I was married briefly before the war. However, the marriage failed through no fault of my own, I cannot be held responsible. My wife and I are now divorced."

I'm thrown by his admission, but it doesn't make any difference whatsoever. Divorce is still rare and frowned upon around here, so no wonder he's kept it a secret.

His shoulders drop, and he runs his hands through his already dishevelled hair with a loud sigh. The fight has suddenly gone out of him.

"Look, I know I've handled the situation badly, even before tonight, Bridie. I've been distracted by thoughts of you these last months, before I invited you to the house even. Of course, I did have an ulterior motive, as my father knew only too well. Who could blame me when you're such an appealing young woman? All I ask is that you give a future with me some thought." His eyes lower to the cobbles. "I'm extremely fond of you, and … and I somehow know I could find it in my heart to love you, if you would only allow me the opportunity."

How many of the girls in the factory would love to be in this position, I wonder. He has such a pleasant face, and I know there are plenty who have a crush on him… and his money. But handsome is as handsome does, as my mother would say.

He knows so little of me, or he would discover that wealth is not at the top of my list. I would not be comfortable with his lifestyle, even if I was madly in love with him. I know my place in society, but I also happen to like it here very much. Not for me fancy dinner parties, and afternoon tea making small talk. I'd rather curl up by the fire with a good book, or while away the hours sewing in quiet companionship with my mother.

Oh, how I want to go home.

Gathering myself together, I take a breath, and decide I have no choice but to put his behaviour to one side.

"Please, Mr Frobisher, I must go," I say, quietly.

I begin walking, and glance over my shoulder to check he isn't following me. He's standing with his shoulders stooped, hands in pockets like a little boy lost, when only moments ago, I was terrified of him.

I can't help thinking now that financial security of any sort will be off the list entirely if my rejection leads to my father losing his job, his reputation, not to mention our home.

And that nightmare would be all my fault because of my inability, or perhaps my unwillingness, to grasp a carrot being dangled right in front of my nose.

Chapter 10

He isn't here. Glancing up and down the path by the crags, there isn't a soul to be seen. That's usual. But I'd expected Henry to be here, waiting on our bench.

My heart plummets. Disappointment takes my breath as I drop my head back to look at the clear summer sky. I've been in church the last three Sundays for the reading of Edyth and Archie's banns and then we've had so many wedding preparations to attend to. We saw the newlyweds off from the station earlier for a week-long honeymoon at Sandsend on the east coast. Neither of them has holidayed before, so they were giddy with excitement in their new 'going away' outfits. Together with my parents, I waved to my brother and new sister-in-law, as the train slowly picked up speed, and then disappeared into the steam of the engine.

My thoughts went quickly then to Henry; he may have been out of sight, but he certainly wasn't out of mind.

I woke with a sickly feeling this morning, worried about coming here, as Elliott Frobisher has discovered my secret. Commonsense however, says he knows now, and it's up to him what he decides to do with the information. In the end, my feet took the walk up the hill for me, as I just couldn't stay away a moment longer.

Perhaps Henry has been waylaid by something unexpected. It must be unexpected as I know otherwise, he would be here. I sit on the bench to wait, but the view isn't calling me for once, my mind preoccupied with the memory of last night, and the whereabouts of my friend. It's a pity, as the weather is the best we've had all summer, the view stretching for miles further than usual. It holds no appeal for me today.

Is Henry just a friend? I admit to being confused after last night's encounter. There's nothing tawdry about my friendship with him, we've done nothing wrong, so why did Elliott Frobisher's words sting so? I'm trying to understand why I feel so protective of him and our friendship, and why I'm sitting here longing for him to appear.

Too many times I glance up the hill, until finally I can stand it no longer, and set off in the direction of Henry's cottage. I know I'm taking us to a different place, I know it, but I just can't go home without seeing him. I pass Mrs Calder's cottage on my right, but there's no sign of her in the garden, or by the window.

If all was well with Henry, he would have come to meet me, I'm certain of it now.

A few hundred yards and I'm over the crest of the crags, where rocks give way to moorland that rushes to meet the sky. The town is no longer visible, and all is still and quiet, except for the gentle shushing of the ever-present breeze. The simple one-storey cottage stands alone, nestled in the heather, almost as if it's trying to hide. At the gate I check for signs of life. There are none, only the sounds of what I think are hens to the rear of the cottage, filling the air. The emptiness is ominous, and I head down the path wondering what I

76

might be walking into. The garden is functional but orderly, the well-tended vegetable beds giving me a flicker of comfort that they haven't been abandoned. The hens cluck madly when they see me, bringing Henry to the door before I knock.

I take a step backwards at the sight of him; in the month since I was last up here, he's not the same man. He's thin and drawn, his eyes dark underneath, sunken. Neither of us say hello, we only stare at each other, until I manage to gather my wits.

"Henry, I'm sorry to just turn up like this, but I was worried. Are you unwell?"

Despite my concern for his welfare, I can't help wondering if I should accept an invitation into his house. The repercussions of our friendship hover around us like a savage dog ready to pounce.

He only stands with the door handle gripped tightly in his hand, perhaps thinking the very same. I know how he worries about the consequences of our meeting up here, because he tells me every time.

"No, it's not me who's ill, Bridie, it's gran. I told you how she's been struggling these months, and now the doctor says …"

His voice cracks on the last word, and he doesn't need to go on. I push the door, and usher him inside the kitchen, glancing around quickly to find a seat. I press a hand on his shoulder when I find a chair by the table, and he drops down on it with his head in his hands. My hand rubs his back, my action seeming inadequate, but I can't think what else to do to soothe him. Poor man, how I hate now to think of him alone up here these last weeks.

I find the kettle; hot, sweet tea is in order, I think, as I put a match to the old stove. I replace the kettle, before rejoining him at the table.

"Is there anything at all I can do to help, Henry?" I ask, taking one of his hands in mine. It's twice as big as my own, and rough from working outdoors. I like the touch of it, and rub my thumb over the back of his hand to soothe him, like my mother would do to me.

He sits staring at our hands a moment until he shakes his head slowly.

"There's nothing to be done, I just need to sit it out and play the waiting game. She's struggling to breathe properly on her own, which means she's sleeping much of the time, but she won't go to hospital. She's never spent a night away from here since she married. I've toyed with the idea of just taking her to hospital, but I … I can't, I'm terrified it will be the end of her either way. Nurse Doris calls every day, and every day it gets harder to watch her leave."

Oh, thank goodness for Nurse Doris, who has been delivering babies and taking care of the sick and elderly for decades, it seems. It's some comfort to know she comes here, so Henry isn't coping entirely alone. She's not the most kindly of souls with her no-nonsense approach to life, but she knows what to do, and she does it well in between visits from the doctor.

My throat seems to be closing, so I can't take any air. I grasp both his hands in mine almost clinging to them, and his grip tightens. Platitudes are not us; we speak honestly, openly, and any hollow words and gestures between us will just not do.

The kettle boiling takes me from my seat to make the tea, searching for the paraphernalia in the dresser drawers and cupboards.

"Have you eaten?" I ask.

He nods, but judging by the state of him, I'm not sure I believe him. There's a pan of what looks like vegetable soup on the hob, so perhaps he had that earlier. Either way, I can't force the man to eat, and I understand how food sticks in your craw when you're worried. The kitchen is much the same as the garden, he's a man who's used to keeping things in order. Archie wouldn't know where to start, but then the two of them have lived very different lives.

"How was the wedding?" he asks suddenly.

"Oh, fine ... nice," I say, not wishing to elaborate when it seems inappropriate.

"You can tell me about it, Bridie, I'd like to hear about the day. It will be a distraction from waiting, and heaven knows, I'd like that." He pauses, gulping a mouthful of tea then stares at me.

"What is it?" I ask.

His eyes lower to the table, and my heart picks up speed.

"I don't like gran being alone long. I know it's a lot to ask, but will you come sit with me on the window seat on the landing? It's just so difficult to be apart from her for long."

"Of course I will," I say quickly, desperately wanting to put an end to his painful explanation.

His sad little smile of gratitude is too much. To think of him up here alone for weeks with this dreadful burden, is enough to make me weep. My throat too tight, I draw air into my nostrils to calm me, as the last thing this man needs right now is me going to pieces.

The staircase is in the far corner of the neat little parlour. At the top, he points to the padded bench under the window, and then disappears into his grandmother's bedroom. Every time he returns to her, he must wonder if she's still with us. What a terrible, terrible thought.

I catch a glimpse of his grandmother's bedroom with its flowered wallpaper and heavy dark wooden furniture. The curtains are swaying in the breeze from the open window, and under different circumstances, I imagine it would be a pretty room. There's a small tumbler of wildflowers on the windowsill that Henry must have brought in from the garden.

I've never been in such a situation before, wondering what my mother would do and say at such a time to guide me.

Henry's voice is muffled before he leaves her room to join me.

"I talk to her all the time," he says, sitting down beside me on the window seat. "Whether she can hear me or not, I can't see as it does any harm."

The bench is so tiny, there's no need to reach to squeeze his arm.

His sigh is heavy, as he turns to me now, saying, "Tell me about yesterday, Bridie, it's a long time since we've been to a wedding. I can tell gran all about it later, it will give me something to talk about."

It's the least I can do, I think. So, I go into elaborate detail describing the dresses, the flowers, the food, conversations, anything I can think of to bring the story to life. I only omit the ending. He sits at my side, his eyes straying occasionally to his grandmother's bedroom door, as I tell him the tale. My only aim is to provide him with some small distraction to his otherwise bleak Sunday.

"Well, it was quite an event, and the wedding of the year by the sound of it," he says when I finish.

I whip my head away from his weary smile, my teeth digging into my lower lip, as I look out at the garden. If things were different, he would have been there, joining in with the fun and festivities. Then the upsetting conversation which took place at the end of the day may never have happened.

He holds out his hand, and I take it, unsure what he means by it. He pulls me up gently from the window seat, saying, "I think I had better let you get back home, Bridie, I've kept you long enough this afternoon."

I can't leave. I sense his grandmother won't be with us next time I see him; the heavy thought of what will become of Henry afterwards tightening my chest. I hold on to his hand and stare down onto his smart little rows of fruit and vegetables.

He drops my hand to bob his head around the door of his grandmother's room, before we return downstairs. I'm strangely lost without its gentle support.

I can't possibly wait a whole week to return, and I tell him as much, as we face each other at the back door.

"You *must* wait," he says, leaning against the dresser. "You'll draw attention to yourself if you don't. There's nothing you can do to help the situation, so there's no point taking the risk. If I didn't have the thought of seeing you to keep me going, life would be worse than it is already."

Oh, that's the wrong thing to say. I'm so close to tears. "But that's just my point. You do have me," I whisper.

Our eyes hold each other, and I take myself unawares when I reach on tiptoe to touch my lips to his cheek. He closes his eyes briefly, before ushering me out of the door, the fresh, clean smell of his skin lingering.

"Go, before I make a complete show of myself," he says, attempting a smile. "I'll see you next Sunday. The thought of that will be a blessing all week."

A week may as well be a lifetime, and I try not to think about what might have happened by then. Seven long days and nights of his grandmother lying there, with little to no food, does not bode well.

I raise my hand to him when I reach the gate, as he watches me through the front window. His desolate smile finally makes the tears I'd held onto so bravely fall freely, as I race back down the hill towards the crag. The sight of the bench seat only increases the flow, and I curse the town for making him struggle up here all alone. Surely, this is a time for compassion for another human being, if nothing else.

But I know it can never be. Old wounds will never heal while people keep picking and broddling them, and it's like a compulsion they just cannot stop.

I sit on the bench and dry my tears with my handkerchief. I must prepare myself for going home and acting as though I've returned from my usual Sunday walk. How shall I ever be able to play the part convincingly with the state I'm in?

At the bottom of the hill, my father is waiting for me, leaning on the front door of the house, smoking a cigarette. My stomach drops at my first silly thought that there might be something wrong with my mother. I take a deep breath that makes my head swim, forcing a smile and a wave as I cross the road.

He doesn't return my wave or show any hint of a smile, and I shiver on a warm day.

That awful expression, so unlike my father, is surely set to be the last thing I see forevermore now, as I fall asleep each night.

Chapter 11

I've been made a prisoner in my own home of late, the cloying atmosphere choking my mood more with each passing day.

The crags now feel like a forbidden place, and the appeal of our once secret garden now tainted. I must not give Elliott Frobisher any opportunity to manipulate me.

I was still recovering from the bittersweet wedding weekend when I returned to work the following Monday. In just two short days, my world had been given a good shake and tipped upside down.

Edyth was away on honeymoon, so at least I wasn't forced to make conversation with her. She would have seen straight through the façade.

Instead, I tried and failed to tune into the lively chatter about the wedding at break time. Everyone agreed it seemed, that it was a unique wedding, the likes of which they would never attend again, and they made a fair point. I was showered with compliments about the beautiful decorations, though the praise failed to lift my mood.

Mr Jarvis was waiting for me that morning, as I trudged up from the canteen. I fought the instinct to bolt like a rabbit as he approached, and when he asked if I would accompany him upstairs to see Mr Frobisher, it took all I had not to weep right there and then in front of the poor, unsuspecting man.

I trailed behind him from the lift, but then we turned left down the corridor towards old Mr Frobisher's room instead. It was preferable, but my relief soon melted to concern, wondering what he could possibly have to discuss with me. Months had passed since he'd discovered me with his son in his sitting room, an oddly shameful memory I'm still keen to forget. I'd hoped then that a stern ticking off from his father might have deterred him, but it only seemed to fuel his obsession.

Mr Jarvis looked nonplussed when Mr Frobisher saw me to a seat by the fireside, though I was just as confused as he was. The weather was too warm for a fire, so a decorative copper fire screen stood before the grate. I fixed my eyes on it, as I waited to hear the reason I'd been summoned.

However, he seemed keen to put me at ease, asking me about the celebrations, and listening, as I gave a potted version of the events of the afternoon after he'd left. Once more, I stopped short of the ending. Perhaps that was the reason he wanted to speak to me, it occurred to me then, my palms growing clammy.

"Well, it sounds like the perfect wedding day, Bridie, I'm so pleased that everything went to plan after all your efforts."

"Thank you, sir," I said. He glanced at my foot tapping frantically, clearing his throat, and I braced myself.

"Bridie, I confess that I've asked you here today for a very … unusual reason, one which you would never guess, I'm sure," he said, sitting back in his wing chair. "It will come as a surprise, but I'm hoping you might be able to help me with a significant problem I'm facing at present, indeed one I've been struggling with for some time."

My face stretched with utter astonishment. What had I, Bridie Foxcroft, to offer a man of his standing?

"Well, as you point out, I'm at a loss to know how I might be of help to you, sir."

He rested his chin on his folded hands and studied me so long I was forced to look away. His pose reminded me of his son.

"Bridie, may I speak candidly to you? I hope I might have your confidence; there's something tells me that you are a girl to be trusted."

My mind went immediately to Henry, and that I wasn't worthy of such an accolade. But then, I reminded myself I had done nothing wrong. Even as I was nodding my agreement, I wasn't keen to add another secret to my list.

"I'm grateful to you for lending an ear and, I hope, a hand," he said, taking a breath. I gripped the arms of the chair, the tension sitting around us. "It's like this you see; since the war, the trading environment has been challenging, shall we say. We are living in times of austerity, and dolls are not the most important item on most people's list of priorities. Even our longest and most loyal customers in the upper echelons are tightening their belts. The world is changing, Bridie."

He paused, looking away, his rheumy eyes full of memory, before returning his mind to the conversation. I understood perfectly well what he was telling me, but I was still at a loss as to how I could help the situation.

"This is only to be expected, and how it should be." He smoothed his hand down his steely hair, still thick with the same wave pattern as his son's. "I've obviously given this a great deal of thought, and I've come to the conclusion we must change as a company, and try something new.

It's all very unsettling to say the least when so many peoples' jobs are a risk. In fact, it keeps me awake at night. But, at my age, I know that in business one must adapt to survive. I'm backed into a corner and need help, and this is where you come in, Bridie." He sat forward so my heart began to pound.

"I confess, I've found myself thinking about the princess dolls you made for your sister-in-law. They are wonderful. I hope you know; truly rare things of beauty, which took my breath away when I saw them. I'm not just saying this to flatter you. I'm sure you have no idea my father started out selling the dolls from a stall in the town market. I worked alongside him as a young boy, and I'm still a salesman at heart. I will always have an eye for what will sell."

His words and manner were genuine enough, the dolls had clearly made an impact on him, and I thanked him for the compliment. He wasn't at all like the intimidating man I'd seen at his home that day.

"They are such a thing of beauty in fact, that I took the liberty of using my contacts, and I have recently been in touch with *Bradley's*, the best toy shop in London. I described the dolls in their exquisite detail, and they think them an innovative idea, much the same as I. The young princess and her sister are obviously much loved and admired, especially since the war. Now, after my conversation with the toyshop, I have a little proposition to put to you."

How I wished he had called for refreshments, as my tongue was glued to the top of my mouth. There were two tumblers and a jug of fresh water on his desk, but I would never have dared ask to take a drink.

"I was wondering, and I know it's a bold request, if they did approve a sample, do you think that with help from your mother, you might be able to dress, say fifty dolls at home over the next six weeks? The conversation with *Bradley's* progressed as we are short on time, and we would need to be ready to include the doll in the toyshop's autumn range." He stared at me as I tried to understand his request. "I know this is unexpected, Bridie ... and a very tall order."

Fifty dolls; why would my silly little creation be stocked in the finest toyshop in London? It was so difficult for me to take in such interest in my gifts for Edyth, and the conversations about them, which had taken place between very important people.

"As I said, I know this is a surprise to you, but I've been considering the option for weeks now. The thing is, if the engagement dolls sell well, then they would like to have a stock of wedding dolls in time for Christmas. They propose a high price point, as the dolls would be exclusive in the first instance, suitable for the gentry. But they could, in theory, be mass produced with sewing machines in the future."

He had clearly made his point well, and his opinion will no doubt be respected in business circles. Like most people, I'd heard of *Bradley's* and seen them in the newspaper, so I knew how well-regarded they were across the country.

Mr Frobisher was waiting for a serious answer to a serious question it seemed, his eager eyes still upon me. I thought then of the practicalities of his suggestion. Fifty dolls were indeed a tall order, but perhaps not impossible with some help, as I had a pattern to work from.

"I am truly honoured you would think of me and my little dolls, sir, believe me," I said. "I'm sure you would provide the materials, so my only worry is time. The outfits are quite intricate to make, as you pointed out yourself."

He nodded quite animatedly then, as though he was starting to get excited by our conversation, saying, "I thought of this, and perhaps you could leave work at lunchtime each day to join your mother at home, and set about the task. It would only be for six weeks, so a short-term solution to begin with." His loud sigh startled me. "To be honest, Bridie, I've no idea if this will work out for us, but I don't see any reason not to try for the modest sums involved in making the doll outfits. The competition from these new plastic dolls is not a passing phase, so we must do something. Surely, it's better to go down fighting than just give up."

His words struck a chord. It seemed that *Frobisher's* was closer to ruin than any of us thought.

I wasn't at all sure if my colleagues would be happy with this new arrangement. Yet, when I thought about it more, what alternative did I have but go along with the plan? I had been asked to carry out a special project by my employer, so I had no choice in the matter. They would do the same in my shoes.

"What should I tell everyone downstairs?" I asked him.

"The truth with regard to the doll order, Bridie. However, I know you understand that there's no need to mention the financial situation of the company. I wouldn't have asked if I didn't think I could count on your discretion."

"Of course, I shan't say a word." I hadn't the heart to tell him that rumours had been rife for months, as they obviously hadn't reached his ears.

"With the extra allowance of time, I'm sure my mother and I can have the dolls ready by autumn," I said, by then almost looking forward to the challenge, with extra sewing time to boot.

"Of course, I shall credit you with their design entirely," he added, and I almost basked in his warm smile.

It should have been one of the proudest days of my life.

"Well, I would be grateful if you could provide me with a list of what you will need before you go," he said. "I shall have Miss Whitehead source them from my contacts, rather than the usual suppliers, to save costs. When they arrive, hopefully tomorrow, I would be grateful if you could sew a sample doll's outfit, and I will personally deliver it to *Bradley's* next week. Perhaps you should mention the plan to your colleagues straight away when you go downstairs, to pave the way forward for us."

It was a relief to know I wouldn't have to lie about the reason for being called upstairs at least.

Miss Whitehead, his secretary, took the short list I'd written on a scrap of paper, as if I'd given her a dirty handkerchief. She probably thinks I've got a little above my station, I thought, as I descended the stairs, rather than waiting for the lift. I wasn't going to risk the door opening to Elliott Frobisher's office.

He is the culprit, though he doesn't know it. He is the one who now has me locked away, unable to see Henry when he needs me the most.

Unbeknown to me, my parents' bedroom window was wide open the night of the wedding due to the hot weather, and my father heard every word of the conversation, as he waited for me to come home from the wedding. There I was, thinking he would be sleeping off the drink, when he was too worried about me getting home safe and sound to be able to sleep.

He wouldn't believe it was true at first, but then a stroll up the hill a little while after I left the following day, soon confirmed the story when he saw me disappear inside Henry's cottage. I was fortunate he didn't decide to act, but apparently, he'd heard about Henry's grandmother being at 'death's door', a turn of phrase that made me wince.

Now, he doesn't want my mother or anyone else to discover my secret. The strain of being in the house is like trying to breathe underwater, and my father's face is telling me he has plenty to say to me in the fullness of time. Unsurprisingly, he's forbidden me to go to the crags, so I don't even know if Henry's grandmother is still with us. All I can do is wait to hear even a whisper of gossip floating around the factory floor each day.

I asked my father if he would find the key, and lock the second gate in the secret garden, the one that leads to the factory yard. How I wanted somewhere to escape to with my thoughts, away from the stifling atmosphere of home. I'd disappointed him for the first time, and I was upset about that as much as everything else.

"I've no idea where the key is, so that's impossible I'm afraid, Bridie. In time, I'm sure you'll be only too glad to sit out there again," he said. His steady gaze left me cold.

I went up to my room and sat looking onto my little haven that may as well have been on the other side of the world, like America, rather than a few feet away.

My father could so easily have barred the gate in some way, even if the key was lost. I understood this was his way of saying he would very much like me to take Elliott Frobisher up on his offer of a courtship, as the lesser of the two evils.

How the tide can change, and how a grudge can make a person behave in such a way you question whether you ever really knew them at all.

Chapter 12

The honeymooners have returned, rested and glowing, with no clue they're now living in a very different house to the one they left. My father may be disappointed in me, but in only a matter of days, the feeling has become entirely mutual.

I gave their room at the rear of the house a good spruce in their absence for something to occupy me, laying their new quilt on the bed as a finishing touch. Their return has lessened the awkward atmosphere a little at least.

Edyth was keen to hear all about the new doll venture, telling me she would be only too happy to help with the accessories, as she's lacking the sewing skills.

A sample doll was personally delivered to *Bradley's* by Mr Frobisher as planned, and they were impressed with the quality enough to honour the order. My employer told me on one of my now regular visits to his office, that he didn't doubt it for a minute. His faith in me is extraordinary.

I've had a little 'ribbing' as my mother calls it from my workmates, but then she says they're only envious. She's brimming with pride, which is heaping on the guilt about the situation with Henry.

I can almost hear him calling me to the crags, and I'm afraid he will think I've deserted him. His broken smile as I left him that day lingers in my thoughts to torture me.

"Have you heard about Henry Friar's grandmother?" Edyth asks, as she arrives home from her shift at the factory.

I catch my breath at the mention of his grandmother, even though I've been waiting for news. Almost three long weeks have gone by without a word about her, and I was foolishly hoping she may have defeated all the odds to make a recovery.

"No, what about her, Edyth? Don't tell me she's passed away, I've heard the rumblings about her being seriously ill," my mother says.

"Yes, it's true, her funeral is tomorrow from what I've just heard at work," Edyth says, splashing cold water on her face at the sink. The August heat is proving to be almost unbearable even in our cotton dresses.

"Oh, now that is sad news," my mother says. "I know what people think of her grandson, but she wasn't to blame, poor woman. These things somehow still always come as a shock, even when we're expecting them."

How right she is, I think, my heart twisting. My mind swims with thoughts and images of Henry, and I drop my head to pretend I'm checking the latest doll's dress in my hands.

"She's been poorly since Christmas by all accounts," Edyth says. "Apparently, she died last week, but the news was slow in reaching us. It's strange how it's taken so long, but then it's like another world up that hill."

My mother puts her sewing to one side, keen to give the conversation her full attention. I carefully pack away my needle and thread, hoping I appear indifferent about the bombshell I've been dreading finally landing in my lap.

"Well, it will be a dismal affair at that funeral tomorrow. I bet there's not a soul turns up to pay their respects," my mother says, her shoulders heaving and falling.

She gets up to fetch the cold cuts of meat from the cellar head to begin arranging them on the platter. It's far too hot to fire up the oven today.

"I'm just going to powder my nose," I say.

They don't notice me sloping out of the room, as they continue their conversation about someone who was nothing but a stranger to us. They're preoccupied with dissecting the life of a woman who was supposedly shamed, but to my mind, did nothing but keep herself to herself and mind her own business.

I kick off my sandals and lay back on the cool eiderdown, allowing the breeze from the open window to float over me. I'm too numb to even weep at the news. Henry will be in his lonely cottage now, waiting for tomorrow like a man on the eve of going to the gallows. He will hate the thought of coming to town, but there's no alternative. That little cottage up the hill must be seeped in misery this night, and I'm powerless to help him.

She was all he had ... and now she's gone.

The tears finally slip down my checks, and I turn to bury my face in my pillow in the hope of stifling the sobs. It's all so unjust, and so unnecessary.

I sit up, frustrated suddenly by my apathy, realising I must not turn my back on Henry and do nothing. I must at least try to get a message to him, as goodness knows what he thinks has happened. Perhaps he thinks I now consider our friendship a risk too far.

Oh, Henry, if only I could just leave the house now and run up to see you. Could I be brave enough? No, I decide, I'm not in a position to rock the boat any further with my father.

By first light, I know sitting on my hands all day is not an option any longer.

When I get to work, I discover the funeral is planned for two o'clock this afternoon. I'm due to be at home working with my mother then, so I could tell her I need to nip back to work for some item or other.

This is exactly what I do at precisely a quarter to two, when I set off down the back track to the church. There's nobody about, as I predicted, because afternoons are generally quieter in town, and people have returned to work after their dinner break by this time. I spot the giant oak at the side of the church, and it makes it quite easy for me to wait out of sight.

At two minutes to two, the funeral car approaches, with Henry and Mrs Calder sitting together in the back seat. I swallow hard more than once, as the funeral director opens the door for them to get out, and there he is.

He looks pale and wan, in what I imagine is his only suit hanging from his frame.

Four unknown men now hoist his grandmother's coffin onto their shoulders in one swift action, as I cling to the broad trunk of the tree for support.

Mrs Calder has her arm in Henry's, as they trail after the coffin in the sunshine, to bid farewell to his beloved grandmother. The bright, sunny weather is not fitting for the occasion, but a rainy day would be worse.

Henry looks ghastly, his eyes even more sunken than the last time I saw him. I doubt he will have slept in weeks, and I wonder who is propping up whom between the only pair of mourners.

They disappear inside the church, and the eerie sound of the organ playing a hymn, drifts outside to join the stillness of the graveyard.

Twenty minutes later, they reappear with the vicar for the burial service, and I bow my head the entire time, hoping Henry somehow senses my support. Mrs Calder holds a handkerchief to her mouth, as Henry wipes his eyes with his own pressed, snow-white handkerchief.

I confess that a sadder sight I have never seen, as I join them in wiping a tear.

They're thanking the vicar and shaking his hand now, when Henry suddenly glances in the direction of the tree. I stick my head out ever so slightly, still unsure if he's spotted me. He keeps his eyes forward as he accompanies Mrs Calder back to the funeral car, helping to settle her inside, before he closes the door.

Turning, he retraces his steps to the tree, and I know now he's seen me waiting for him. Our eyes never leave each other, my heart racing so I can barely catch the warm air to breathe.

Finally, after being kept apart without our consent for weeks, we find ourselves alone.

He glances over his shoulder, saying, "I'm grateful to you for coming, Bridie, more than you will ever know, but you must go home now before somebody sees you." He glances over his shoulder yet again, and I think of all the times I used to do the same.

The shame of the memory makes me drop my eyes to the dry grass.

"I'm so sorry about your grandmother, Henry. I've let you down, but believe me, I would have done anything for things to be different. I've thought of nothing else but you up there in your cottage, trying to cope alone." He opens his mouth, but I put up my hand. "It's just that my father discovered I'd been seeing you. It's a long story, but he was waiting for me the last Sunday that I saw you and ... and he's none too pleased with me."

His hand goes to his mouth, his eyebrows disappearing under the peak of his black cap. "Oh, Bridie, you've no idea about the dark thoughts I've had these last weeks. I've been a fool, I should never have doubted your integrity as a friend," he says, reaching to lightly touch my forearm. I place my hand on top of his, sinking into the comfort it gives me, hoping it gives him the same.

"Never doubt it," I say, "I had to come today, no matter what."

He searches my face, his hand tightening his grip.

"It must be terrible at home. Has your father told your mother?"

"No, nobody knows but Elliott Frobisher, and now my father, but that's a story for another time," I say. "Henry, we don't have much time. Tell me, what do you intend to do now?"

His eyes go to Mrs Calder waiting in the car. We're well hidden still behind the tree, but the threat of being discovered is always with us.

"I know I ought to leave here now that gran's gone, it would be in my best interests ... but there's someone stopping me."

We stare at each other under the dappling leaves of the tree. I know what I need and want to do without a second's hesitation.

Placing my hand to his cheek, I press my lips on his firmly, confidently as though I've done it many times before. His arms go around me, and he clings to me as our kiss goes on and on, my arms tightly woven around his neck. I'm so lost in the unexpected pleasure of it, the passion telling me that we're far more than friends.

"Get your filthy bloody hands off her, Friar."

My father's voice breaks the spell. His tone is disturbingly quiet, but then Henry is pulled from my arms, and I let out a small squeal when he's pushed to the ground.

I'm frozen with shock until I come to my senses, tugging at my father's arm. "Da, please, he's just buried his grandmother. Leave him alone out of respect for her, if nothing else."

"I just knew you'd come here," he hisses, as Henry jumps to his feet, his suit covered in dust from the dry ground. "Go home, Friar, and leave my daughter alone if you care anything for her at all. She's right, I'll not hit a man on a day such as this, so you're damn lucky, I can tell you that much."

Henry holds his cap in his hand, still paying respect to my father, even when I'm not certain he deserves it. "I'm sorry to upset you, Mr Foxcroft," he says adjusting his tie. "But I care for your daughter very much, and rightly or wrongly, I know she feels the same."

My father makes a grab for Henry's jacket but he's too quick, taking a step backwards so my father grabs nothing but air. Blind fury is making his cheeks burn, as he stands with his arms hanging by his sides.

Henry turns to me now, saying, "Bridie, I should go. You know, the last thing I ever want is to cause trouble for you."

Before I can answer him, he strides away, down the church pathway to return to the car and Mrs Calder. He leaves me feeling exposed and alone, wanting so much to chase after him. I know I may never see him again if he leaves town, because I'll never find out where he's gone. I wrap my arms tightly around my body until my father grabs my arm. He pulls me towards the pathway at the rear of the church, and I try to release my arm, thinking of Elliott Frobisher and his bullying that night.

"Da, you're hurting me, stop it. I'll come of my own accord," I tell him.

Dropping his hand, he leans against the dry-stone wall, breathless. He looks up towards the cloudless sky, the sunshine pouring into every line of his face.

"Why, Bridie, of all the people you could have taken up with, why did you have to pick him? He's a coward and he always will be. How can you care for a man such as him? You were raised better than that, by God but you were."

He rolls his head from side to side, closing his eyes, as though he's in pain at the thought of Henry and me together.

"You don't know him, da, or the first thing about his life. He's a good man. The war is over, it has been for five years. I just know that there's more to it, but in any case, his reserved status was accepted, so who made you and the rest of the townspeople judge and jury."

His face flies in my direction, the disgust in his eyes making me look away.

"What good reason could there be for not stepping up to fight for your king and country, your own family even? We all could have shunned our duty, but we didn't, and many paid the price with their lives, or by living as a shadow of their former selves, like some men still are today. That is *not* a farm up there; he is *not* a farmer. I won't have it, Bridie, I will not have you take up with him, do you hear me?"

His raised voice startles me when I've never heard it before today. Somehow, I manage to gather courage to face his look of fury head on, though I'm quaking,

"No, but you would have me take up with a man who blackmailed me, a man who I don't love," I say, my chest heaving like I've been running for miles.

"Love … what do you know about love?" he says, his top lip snaking into a sneer. "Talk of love is for romance books and silly little girls. As for Mr Frobisher, what choice do we have in the matter? You could lose your job, I could lose mine, even Edyth. Then there's our home, the roof over our heads; you know full well what's at stake. Oh, and not to mention breaking your poor mother's heart if she found out about you and Friar."

I close my eyes to the facts that I knew well enough before they were hammered home for me, a tear dropping onto my dress. My father sighs, stepping closer to place a hand gently on my arm this time.

"He's not a bad man, lass," he says flatly.

For one mad second I think he's talking about Henry, and my heart lifts just a little.

"You know, you could even grow to love him in time."

I take a step backwards, staring at my father as though he's lost his mind. He brazens it out, staring back at me until he can stand it no more. He turns to walk ahead of me, and storm down the pathway so we can return to a place that is no longer my home. I've only just realised just how much I detest being inside those four walls nowadays.

I shake my head. Love is for books, he says.

He basks in the glow of it every day with my mother, yet he would deny me, his own daughter, a single drop of it.

Chapter 13

"Well, I'd be obliged if you would no longer keep us in suspense, Elliott," Mr Frobisher says, attempting to keep his tone light and jovial for the rest of us. "Everyone else is in agreement, so I can't for the life of me see why you wouldn't be."

The princess engagement dress dolls have sold out. They flew off the shelves far quicker than expected, and now there's a waiting list of nearly seven hundred as of today. It's barely the middle of September; we could never have imagined being in such a position less than a month ago. The waiting list total for the bride doll sits at over a thousand, so plans must be made to employ a team of seamstresses to make the dolls in time. We have two months to get them finished, and that will be cutting it fine. The dresses are tiny but intricate, and I need to train the new starters to bring them up to scratch with the specifications. The final order for machines and materials is waiting to be placed today, along with the advertisement for the jobs in the newspaper.

And the only reason Elliott Frobisher is stalling, is purely and simply because of his so-called affection for me.

I still grip Edyth's hand under the table. She has been such a help, working out quantities and costings, and we've fed back the information to Mr Frobisher regularly, looking at different ways to cut costs without the quality suffering. Our wages have increased, and they're set to increase even further after today. Perhaps a little house to rent for Edyth and Archie might not be out of the question after Christmas, much sooner than they hoped.

Elliott Frobisher would be wise to remove his look of disdain or risk the investors at the meeting wondering what on earth is going on, and coming to their own conclusions. They've asked so many questions, needing to be reassured about the health of the order book and our ability to keep the stores supplied. They were a bit sceptical at first—one of them said that investing in porcelain dolls would be pouring money down the drain—but after old Mr Frobisher worked his charm on them, and the sales came flying in, they couldn't get their cheque books out quick enough.

But a wrong word from Elliott Frobisher could sink us before we've even got going properly.

He takes a sip of water, making sure he prolongs his moment of power.

"Well, everything seems to be in order," he says. "Although the solution to our problem is a trifle irregular, I agree that at least on paper, it appears to be the best way forward for the company."

There was nothing he could say to the contrary without looking a complete fool, because the business proposal is exactly as he described it.

Quiet applause ripples around the table, and Edyth pulls me to her side in a shared moment of joy. The plan will secure the future of this long-established business for the foreseeable, and then who knows for how much longer. I spoke to Mr Frobisher about the possibility of making one style of dress per season from the princess's wardrobe collection, after the popularity of the celebration dolls wane. He says he intends to expand the range over the course of the next five years. The possibilities for *Frobisher's Doll Emporium* are now endless ... and all because of a silly, little gift.

If I glance in the direction of Elliott Frobisher, my delight will evaporate quicker than the morning mist. I'm on the cusp of bursting into tears, the awful tension within me threatening to expose itself at the wrong moment. It's as though I've been walking on broken glass for weeks since the funeral. For all I know, Henry may well have packed up and moved away after the altercation with my father, even if only to improve life for me. I haven't heard a whisper of it yet, so this is the only thing that gives me hope.

"I think now would be the perfect time to thank Bridie, Miss Foxcroft, for the idea, and making the original dolls. I'm sure her sister-in-law would agree they make the perfect gift," Mr Frobisher says, his face beaming like a proud father.

Edyth and I share a wide smile as the Board mutter their agreement with, "Here, here," and I feel my cheeks burn, as I glance around the long table at the admiring expressions.

Everyone that is, except one person who has a face like a spoilt, sulking child.

"So, I shan't keep you gentleman any longer," Mr Frobisher says. "I know you have a long journey back to London, and I thank you for taking this extra trip to see us. My son and I have much to do if we are to make this opportunity a reality."

Edyth and I stand, and the gentlemen shake our hands warmly on their way out of the boardroom.

Elliott Frobisher is the first to leave, striding off in my peripheral vision to sit and stew alone in his office, no doubt.

As Edyth and I join the end of the line, I realise I'm quivering from head to toe, my dinner from only two hours ago curdling in my stomach.

"Well, that was exciting, wasn't it?" Edyth says, on the way down the stairs.

"Yes, very exciting," I say, but my tone lacks enthusiasm when I should be as giddy as she is.

She stops and turns to me at the bottom of the staircase, so I almost collide into her.

"Bridie, are you quite sure you're alright? I know there's been so much change since the wedding, but you really don't seem yourself at all these days."

I stare at the stone flags, thinking how to answer without telling lies, so I can nip her concerns in the bud.

"I'm fine, honestly, Edyth, just a little tired that's all. It's been a tall order, but we pulled it off," I say too brightly. My bottom lip trembles at the first lie, so I must bite it.

She reaches for my hand, and I pull it away sharply or risk crumpling in a heap.

"That's it, I've had enough," she says. "Come on, miss, let's go into the ladies. Mr Jarvis will think we're still upstairs."

I have no alternative now but to allow her to lead me by the arm to duck into the ladies' toilets. She checks each cubicle to satisfy herself that we're alone, then plants me on the low windowsill.

"Right, what's going on with you? And please don't say nothing, or I think I might just push you out of the window."

Her attempt at humour is lost on me, as I continue to shake. I've been running on my nerves these past weeks, and now the deal has been settled, even those are lost to me.

I lean my head against the wall by the window and decide if I can say the words aloud. Edyth is watching me like a bird of prey, taking in every tick of my expressions.

"I've fallen in love with the wrong person," I whisper.

She blows out a long breath, standing perfectly still a moment, one hand on her hip. Finally, she moves a strand of hair from my forehead, pressing her palm softly against my cheek. My teeth dig further into my lower lip.

"Bridie, I can tell you this much, love is never wrong. Who are you in love with, Elliott Frobisher? I've seen the way he looks at you, pretending he hates you when he's fooling nobody. I should think every member of the Board knows it after that meeting."

I pull some distempered air into my nostrils and close my eyes. For once, I think it would be better if I could be in love with him.

I shake my head slowly.

She drops her hand, and I look into her trusting eyes, knowing it will change everything if I should tell her my secret.

"You won't like it, Edyth, I can tell you that much. I shouldn't be telling you, but I'm losing my mind, and you know me too well."

"Look, you're starting to worry me now. Just tell me; is he married, is that it?"

"It's Henry Friar."

The words are out, like a poisoned dart hurtling towards her. They hit the target, and she clamps both hands to her mouth.

"No, Bridie, anybody but him. Not Henry Friar, your da and Archie will never forgive you if they find out," she says between her fingers.

The way she says Henry's name cuts me to the quick, so I'm unable to respond at first. Somehow, it sounds so much worse coming from Edyth.

"Unfortunately, my father does know, as does Elliott Frobisher. He's using the knowledge to blackmail me into taking up with him. Oh, Edyth, it's all such a terrible mess, and I haven't a clue what to do."

She sits by my side on the windowsill, her face white, as though all the lifeblood has been drained from her. It's too late for regrets, the words can never be unspoken, and I just can't see how I could hide the secret forever.

We sit shoulder to shoulder, me with one eye on the door, as I tell her the whole sorry tale. Edyth was always the first person I told any news after I told my mother. This time however, I'm not sure if I will be able to make her understand how I feel, or even why I feel as I do. She will only be able to see Henry through the same eyes as the whole town.

"It would be in your best interests to forget him, Bridie. He'll move away, I'm sure of it now his grandmother has gone. Nobody would want to stay somewhere they're hated." She pauses, placing a hand on mine. "I'm sorry, but it must be said. He made his own bed."

Jumping up from the sill I glare down at her, as her eyes shoot my way. I was right, I could never make her understand, and I was foolish to think otherwise.

"Would it be in my best interests to forget him, or everyone else's, I wonder, Edyth. I'll tell you this much, if he leaves then I'll go find him. I'll be looking for him the rest of my life if needs be. That's only what you would do with our Archie, that's what love does to a person, I understand now."

Our eyes lock a moment, and I watch the workings of her mind without knowing what they mean. Her shoulders finally drop with a sigh, then she stands to draw me into her arms. I rest my head on her shoulder, feeling a sense of peace for the first time in months. I've been worried about losing her love and trust as much as my family's.

"Oh, Bridie, are you sure he feels the same even? I wonder if you've had a conversation about the future, because you could be ruining your reputation, and your life for nothing in the end."

I nod, my head still on her shoulder, too weary to lift it. I've known how he feels since the first time I saw the bench seat waiting for me. If he'd carved our names in the wood on it, he could not have been made it any plainer to me.

"Then we must tread carefully," she says quietly, almost to herself. "Your mother finding out would be bad enough—it's a good job she's too distracted at the moment—but if Archie found out, then who knows what he might do. He is your big brother after all, and very protective of you."

Grasping my arms tightly around her back, I cling to her. Edyth has a way of making me believe everything will turn out fine just by her presence.

"I'm sorry for telling you, Edyth, I sometimes forget you're not just my best friend any longer," I say, lifting my head to look at her.

"No, I'm your family," she says, our arms still around each other's shoulders. "You've a heart of pure gold, Bridie Foxcroft, and I know you well enough to understand you wouldn't give it to just anybody, so whatever that man may be, he must have something good about him."

I'm certain her words will stay with me forever. They were spoken with perfect timing by someone I admire so much.

The comfort they bring is short-lived, however, when I realise that she's only been married two minutes, and I've already placed a secret between her and her new husband.

Chapter 14

The days are shorter and turning chillier, and my time is now spent by the fire, wondering what ploy Elliott Frobisher will come up with next to see me. The calm is ominous, unsettling me further, and I sense something is afoot.

His options are limited now, as I'm either at home under the watchful eye of my father, or at work under the protective eye of his. Mr Frobisher may have thought his son was intimidating me or, more likely, that I'm not of the correct breeding and standing to make a union. Either way, I'm grateful for the shield he provides.

"I was thinking of taking a walk for some fresh air this afternoon, Bridie, if you'd care to join me," Edyth asks as we dry the dishes. "I love autumn, and the snow will be here soon enough, so we'll be stuck indoors much more."

My father glances in our direction but returns to reading his paper when, as far as he's aware, Edyth knows nothing of my situation with Henry. Archie has taken to his bed, sleeping off his Sunday dinnertime drinking session.

Excitement and fear wash over me in a powerful if confusing wave; she has thrown me a lifeline, and my heart races now at the thought of the unexpected afternoon ahead.

"Yes, that would be nice, Edyth, I'd like that," I say, hoping my tone is level enough to disguise my mixed feelings.

When we leave the house behind a little while later, the two of us chat about work until we're well out of earshot. I glance over my shoulder to see if my father is watching out of the window, but he's nowhere to be seen, and my shoulders drop. The relief of being out of captivity flows freely, as I link my arm through Edyth's.

"Well, this has taken me by surprise," I say to her. "I just can't thank you enough, as the day ahead was looming." She doesn't respond, so I continue babbling. "Goodness knows what I'll find when I get to Henry's cottage, but I'm so desperate to see him after all this time."

She stops walking, turning to me with cheeks flushed from the climb already.

"I must be honest with you, Bridie, I'm not at all sure if we're doing the right thing here. All I do know is that I keep equating it to how I would feel in your predicament. I can only think it to be torture, waiting and worrying with your future in other people's hands."

I shrug, raising my eyebrows at her frank assessment of the situation.

"I think perhaps doing something is better than doing nothing at all, at least," I say.

I'm keen not to waste this precious time I've been gifted, tugging her arm to continue our journey up the hill.

"I promise, I shan't dawdle when … if I see him. You know I'd do the same for you, Edyth, if the shoe was on the other foot."

Her tight-lipped smile shows me she knows it's the truth, as she follows me up the crags.

I proudly show her the bench seat before she sits on it to borrow my view of the town for a while.

"See you soon," she says, pulling a book from her bag. "It looks to me to be the perfect spot to sit on a sunny autumn afternoon."

As I leave her, the freedom of being up here with the wind on my face is chasing me. I could almost allow myself a moment of happiness, if I only knew for certain Henry would be waiting for me.

Everything looks and sounds the same as the last time I was here, but now I'm wracked with nerves for very different reasons. I mustn't dilly dally and take advantage of Edyth's kindness, so I hurry down the pathway to the back door.

I spot Henry before I reach it, head bent and tugging what will surely be the last carrot of season from the ground to add to the pile by his side.

"Henry," I say.

He looks up from his task, sitting back on his haunches and shaking his head, as though he thinks his mind might be toying with him. His skin, still tanned from the summer sunshine, shows how much he's been outdoors these last weeks. I forgot how appealing he is to look at with his broad shoulders, and strong arms under his rolled-up shirt sleeves.

"You're late," he says, still hunkered on the ground.

Slowly, I walk towards him, despite everything, unable to help a small smile. He brushes the soil from his hands, and when he stands, he towers above me. He touches my cheek with his thumb just like the day of the funeral, and it sends the same tingle down my back. His hands are becoming my most favourite part of this man. My smile disappears as I look into the depths of his reassuring eyes. I can only hear birdsong as I reach to run my fingers through his thick curls and pull his head down to mine. Our lips touch gently, then less so, as he draws his body nearer.

"God, I've missed you," he says between kisses, his breath warm on my face. Everything about Henry from his skin to his soul is clean and pure, I realise now. "I've been waiting. I'm still here because I knew you'd find a way to come; I just knew it. I couldn't turn the key in the lock for the last time while ever I had hope."

His heart is pounding against mine; it thrills me that I'm doing this to him just by being close to his body.

"I don't have much time, but I think we should go inside," I say, squealing with delight when he picks me up to carry me into the house, still kissing me with every step. He sits me on the table, and I shrug my arms out of my coat. I've been pining for him, yearning almost for his touch since the day in the churchyard, and before even.

My hands go to his chest, and I bury my face in the softness of the hairs peeping from the top of his shirt where the buttons are undone.

I try to draw him closer to me, gasping when he suddenly pulls away to pace the kitchen floor.

"Stop, Bridie, we must stop before we go too far."

Every part of me is crying out for him, and the strain of his trousers tells me he feels the same. Oh, Henry, I think, it's the measure of you that you care more for me than your own needs. Jumping down from

114

the table I lay my head on his chest until his arms slide around me.

"I've missed you too," I mumble into his shirt. His scent is of the outdoors, and it may as well be the finest cologne. "I'm a little overcome at having the opportunity to see you so unexpectedly. Edyth is waiting for me on our bench, so I mustn't keep her waiting long. I hope I might come again, but what I really want to say to you is, please don't go anywhere, Henry, I don't know what I would do if you left, not now."

His arms tighten around my back, his chin dropping onto my hair.

"I should leave," he says. "It would avoid a bucket-load of trouble, and you know it too. I've thought about it every day but somehow, I can't be without you near me. Even if we can never be together properly, I'd settle for this the rest of my days."

I close my eyes, hoping I will be able to recall how I feel this moment when I'm laid awake, fretting about our future.

"How have you been managing?" I ask.

His sigh wafts my hair; reality has swiftly returned, but time is of the essence. I can't add, "Up here all alone," as it's too stark a truth to spell out for both of us.

"I've been doing some work in the village where I sell my produce. It's been a blessing for keeping my hands, if not my mind occupied." He pulls away to look at me, his palms still circling my arms. "Tell me the latest news about Elliott Frobisher, I must know before you go."

That man's name has a habit of making my heart thud every time I hear it.

"He's taken a liking to me and wants to stake his claim. I'm doing all I can to give him a wide berth," I say, mindful to keep a lightness to my tone. Now is not the time to go into detail and add to Henry's endless concerns.

"I bet he does," he says. He smiles, but he doesn't convince me. "And here's little old me standing in the way of your secure future. I should step aside and let you have it."

My hand reaches to touch his cheek, but he can't hold my eyes. I wait for more than a few seconds until he's ready to look at me. He must see the truth; I must make him see the truth or he might do what he sees as the honourable thing, and leave town.

"Well, I can put your mind at rest about that at least. He's the last person I'd take up with, and I'm afraid he knows it, because I've been forced to tell him. It seems he won't take no for an answer and keeps trying to get me on side because he knows the power he has over me and my family. It only lowers my opinion of him."

Henry's laugh is low and hollow. "Believe me, I can understand well enough. Rich or poor, any man would feel lucky to have you, Bridie. You're a rare thing in this dreary world."

I drown in his eyes a moment, seeing exactly what Edyth needed to be convinced of. His love for me shines brightly. "Well, in that case you've won the dip. I'm all yours, Henry. Friar. If you didn't know before today, I think it's time to tell you that … that I love you."

His shy smile strengthens the feeling that sprouted a long time ago, beating down on me each day like warm sunshine between the clouds.

"I loved you the day you appeared on the hill, even before you saw me," he says. "I sometimes caught sight of you deep in thought, staring at the view. I never dared hope you might one day feel the same. There are plenty of people down in that town who have ruined my reputation."

"There are, but they know nothing. One day I'll find out why you were so adamant to walk into a different kind of firing line. From where I'm sitting, it's far from the easy way out. It's a life sentence of its own."

He takes my hand, and I somehow know for certain that he will tell me the moment he's good and ready, whenever that may be.

"I can't believe Edyth has done this for us, what a kindness. Do you think she will be your decoy again?" he asks, his eyes sparkling with hope.

"I really have no idea to be honest, Henry, I know it wasn't easy for her. I'm having to take one day at a time, and it upsets me that she's in the middle of all this. It might not be next week, but I hope it won't be too long before I can see you again."

Nodding, his eyes glisten, and I reach to press my lips to his in a kiss that must last us for who knows how long. This time it's the gentlest touch of a farewell … for now.

Grabbing my coat from the table where I discarded it in careless abandon only moments ago, I head to the open door.

"So, until we meet again," he says, his face unsmiling.

The room disappears as I stare at him, soaking up every detail I can to take away with me while I'm waiting for our next encounter.

At the gate I wave to him, rushing now back down the hill. This time however, I couldn't be more certain about my love.

Edyth is sitting on the bench with her book on her lap. She has been distracted, lapping up the view of our house that drew me up here in the first place. I place my hands on her shoulders and join her in looking at it together, trying to draw some peace from my sister.

She holds my hand on her shoulder, dropping her chin to it, in such a loving gesture I think I could be sick with guilt. That happy little home is no more, though half the people in it don't even know.

Heaven knows what will become of us all, as there can be no turning back for me.

Not now.

Chapter 15

Mr Frobisher follows his son past the line of workers on the ground floor, and out of the front door. They're both walking at speed, and for once, Elliott Frobisher doesn't even bother to look the side I'm on. My stomach knots, but for a different reason this time.

I came down from upstairs to check all was in order with the new machinists, to see yet more drama unfolding. Something is wrong at the Frobisher house, I know it.

Only moments ago, the telephone rang when I was with Mr Frobisher in his office. I had been showing him the quality of the sewing from the new seamstresses, and I could tell immediately by the drop of his face that trouble was afoot. The faint voice of his son hummed down the telephone line, the conversation brief, but then afterwards Mr Frobisher sat very still staring at his desk for a long second. I fiddled with the tiny doll's dress in my hand, as I waited in the silence for him to remember I was there.

"I'm sorry, Bridie, but I must cut our meeting short." He paused, and I jumped to my feet, glad to be freed from the awkward moment that had descended upon us. "I'm afraid there's something I must attend to at home."

I wasn't hoping for an answer when I said, "I hope all is well. Good afternoon, sir," grabbing the rest of the sewing samples to make a hasty retreat.

His voice followed me, saying, "Good afternoon, Bridie. All will be resolved in due course, no doubt. As for the sewing, if you're happy with the quality, then so am I. You're the expert, as I keep telling everyone."

My smile was lost on him, as he was already sliding into his coat, clearly keen to get home.

We've had the pick of the finest seamstresses for miles around, and the dolls have lost none of their qualities from being produced in huge quantities. The orders are on schedule, and *Frobisher's* has been featured recently in the newspapers. We've already received plenty of orders from the smaller toy shops.

Mr Frobisher took me by surprise last week when he gave me fifty shares in the company. I signed the paperwork, simply in awe of his faith in me, and the lengths he was prepared to go to so he could express his gratitude to me. I suspect I will be earning more than Mr Jarvis in the not-too-distant future, though perish the thought he might discover it.

I have seen Henry only once in the last month. I've been longing to see him, but we agreed that neither of us would want to push our luck and take liberties with Edyth's good nature.

"You're quite the little businesswoman," Henry said, when I told him of my good fortune at the factory. "It sounds as though you've saved their bacon at the eleventh hour, mind you."

"I would say luck and fate have had a lot to do with it," I told him.

I'm happy not to have money troubles on my mind along with everything else. Securing my father's job, and of course our house that goes with it, has been a great relief.

That Sunday when Edyth was our decoy, I made my unspoken decision not to include her in our future plans. It was too much of a risk, one which made me uncomfortable, and she had her marriage to think of.

The winter months stretched ahead like a never-ending road, so I needed inspiration about how I might see Henry. Needs must as they say, and my need had become powerful and distracting.

My father has little to say to me nowadays, unless the rest of the family are around, but I'm almost growing used to it. He's always very cunning when my mother is with us, so she doesn't suspect any unrest between us.

I've been thinking about renting a small flat in town to have more freedom to come and go as I see fit. I'm well over twenty-one now, and I can afford it quite easily since the increase in my wages. I had to find a plan for my sanity, and I did. My plan is to sit tight at home until after Christmas to not upset my mother, then look for somewhere suitable to rent nearby.

Once, leaving home before I married would have been unthinkable, but life is so different now. Edyth and Archie are of the same mind about moving out in the New Year, so my parents will be living alone after years of watching over their brood.

The dark shadow looming over my plan is Elliott Frobisher. He remains forever on the prowl, watching, stalking me like prey. He may not be able to blackmail me with telling my father any longer, but there's still the rest of the town, not to mention my mother and Archie. If the man should finally seize the moment and ask my father for my hand in marriage, I know he will feel he's not in a position to refuse.

At home time, Edyth and I leave together as usual, and I mention the sudden departure of the two Mr Frobishers. I just happened to be in the wrong place at the wrong time, but she shakes her head at me, completely in the dark, as they both left by the lift.

"Tell me more," she says, walking in time with me on the cobbles.

"That's just it, I can't think what could have happened, but it all seemed very drastic whatever it is," I say as I follow her through the back gate to our garden. It's always open nowadays, so we may as well take advantage of the shortcut.

My mother is removing her overall when we go in, ready for my father's return. She's always kept herself smart and well turned out, though she has no interest in the latest fashions.

"Hello, ladies, tea won't be long. What a to-do there's been at the factory today," she says, combing her hair in the mirror over the mantle. "Your father was telling me all about it on his afternoon break." She returns to the table and reaches for the bread to slice. "I just can't believe it, can you?"

Edyth and I wash our hands, then sit down to butter the slices of bread my mother has cut into doorsteps. We have our little routines nowadays, and we soon find an easy flow.

"It sounds as though you're in the know more than us, mam, to be honest. What did da have to say about the drama at the house?"

Edyth and I share a glance as we work in time, piling the bread on the plate.

My mother rolls down her sleeves and buttons the cuffs of her dress to complete her little end-of-day ritual.

"Well, I thought you'd all know about the unexpected turn of events by now. I doubt young Mr Frobisher could ever have foreseen it though," she says, with a faraway look in her eye. I think I might burst with curiosity if she doesn't spit it out. "It seems his wife has returned from America today. As I live and breathe, she sits in their home this evening, as bold as brass."

Edyth's gasp joins my own in the quiet kitchen. My mother pulls a chair out to sit down with us at the table and complete our little circle of gossip.

"Joseph has been driving to and from the Frobisher house since this morning, and there's been such a drama unfolding there by all accounts. It seems young Mr Frobisher discovered that his wife didn't leave on her own when she left him. She was with an American serviceman she met in London when her husband was away. A fine way to carry on, if you ask me, when your husband's putting his life on the line." She sniffs her disapproval. "I suspect young Mr Frobisher never expected her to darken his doorstep again, and I can only think she must have been in dire straits to put herself through such an ordeal. From what I remember back then, she didn't seem to be in his life for two minutes before she left him. I only ever saw her from a distance, but your father said she was the kind of woman who would never be satisfied with her lot. He said it before she upped and left, so everybody in town wondered where she'd disappeared to."

Edyth slumps back in her chair, dropping her butter knife on the plate. "So that's where she ran away to, I would never have guessed it. The rumours that have been flying around over the years would make your toes curl."

"I've heard them myself," my mother says, leaning into the circle. "I'd even heard she was murdered at the hands of her husband or some such nonsense. Of course, I never believed a word of it. My way of thinking is that the serviceman has left her in the lurch by the look of it, or she surely wouldn't have left a glamorous life in America behind to return to Halifax."

"It might not have been as glamorous as we think," Edyth says. "We only see what the films show us at the pictures. They'll be living their lives much the same as us, but with better weather, I imagine."

I'm barely listening; so, Mrs Frobisher has returned with her tail between her legs, perhaps to beg her husband's forgiveness. A glimmer of light appears for me, and it's beginning to shine brighter by the second.

"Well, I never," I say. The light dims slightly when I remember what Elliott Frobisher told me on the night of the wedding. "I wonder what will happen, as I hear they were divorced. He isn't forced to take her back, especially if she was unfaithful to him."

My mother gets up to stir the stew on the stove, tasting it before adding a touch more salt and pepper, and then a small cotton sack of herbs from the garden.

"No, that's true enough, he isn't forced to," she says, rejoining our little huddle. "However, according to Joseph, he might need to reconsider, as she's returned with a young boy in tow. His wife must have been having a baby when she left, as Joseph told your father that the boy is unmistakably Mr Frobisher's son, *and* he's the right age. There can be no denying it even if he wanted to. Apparently, the whole town will be in agreement when we see him, so there will be no chance of her husband, former or otherwise, being able to shirk his responsibilities in polite society.

At least, not if the man knows what's good for him, and his future."

Chapter 16

Christmas is now less than seven weeks away. Bonfire night has come and gone, so my mother is in full swing with her preparations for the festive season. The cake has been made and soaked daily in brandy for a week, cards have been bought from the newsagents, and even the Christmas chutney is sitting in wait on the pantry shelf.

Ordinarily, I would be joining in wholeheartedly with the preparations. I enjoy this time of year above any other, but I have too many other concerns dominating my time and energy.

I caught sight of the mysterious Mrs Frobisher last week when she walked past the newsagents holding her young son's hand. My father is right, the young boy, James, is the spitting image of his father. I assumed they were heading to the shops, and I thought about what my mother said about how small her life must seem now, compared to the one she's left behind. I doubt America is all Hollywood glamour, but I'm sure it will have had a little more to offer than our small town, and the isolation of the Frobisher house.

She looked out of place in a black coat with a brown fur collar, and matching fur hat. The outfit was smart, but far too grand to be walking the streets of Halifax on a weekday morning. Her golden waves falling from beneath her hat, and her freckled nose, were very pretty, though her complexion was ghostly pale against her dark coat.

Oh, how I hope her husband is being kind to them both, but who can say what goes on behind closed doors? My experience of his other side was not pleasant, and I should not like a child to witness such behaviour.

I wondered about the airman, and whether he may have assumed he was the father of her child, having never seen her husband in person. Whatever the stories both men have been told, her lies have left a terrible mess in their wake, for both her and their son.

The events at the house have made me even more aware of how my life is in danger of exploding at any moment should my relationship with Henry be discovered. The debris would then float around me for years to come, much the same as for Mrs Frobisher, who's still living amongst it after so long.

Any opportunity to see Henry before or during Christmas will be out of the question, so seeing him again seems so very far away.

Today is the 10th of December, a Friday. I stand at the front window looking up at the crags, the weekend looming, when once I used to look forward to it. The bell would signal the end of the day at the factory, and I'd rush home with my pay packet to tip up my board money for my mother. Then, all that was left to do, was to wait and see what delights were on offer for tea. Those days of contentment seem long ago now.

As I stare at the crags, already twinkling with frost in the early twilight, an idea appears from nowhere. At first it seems ludicrous and too much of a risk, but then a plan slowly begins to form. Each stage of the plan steadily falls into place in my mind until I'm convinced that I just might be able to carry it out.

Friday and Saturday evenings are usually heavy drinking sessions for the men at the *Feathers*. My father and brother disappear to fall in with the doors at seven o'clock sharp, whilst my mother and I sew, and Edyth tends to indulge in a book or a magazine.

It's a particularly cold Friday evening and I'm trying to lose myself in the repetition of the new rag rug we're trying to finish in time for Christmas. We'll place it in front of the freshly black-leaded range, gleaming in preparation for the festivities. This was a habit my mother picked up from my grandmother, and placing the rug by the fire after the tree is decorated is a little tradition we now have in our house.

We have two sherries each on a Friday and Saturday evening, "For medicinal purposes," as Edyth quips, and they ensure we sleep like logs. Tonight, I pour the measures and only have one; I must stay alert for the plans that lay in wait.

The three of us head up to bed at half past ten, but I don't undress, only settling down to anticipate the long hour until the men arrive home from the pub. They'll have eaten fish and chips on the walk back, and they always come straight up to bed. Then they fall into a drink-filled sleep, usually within minutes of their head hitting the pillow. I often hear their snoring drifting down the landing.

I sit by the window overlooking the garden with just my frantic thoughts for company. The planters that are now dusted with snow are a beautiful sight in the moonlight, if only I was in a calm enough frame of mind to enjoy it.

Being creatures of habit, the men arrive home right on cue, but I decide to wait another half an hour before I make a move. I think it best to be sure my mother and Edyth are sound asleep.

But the delay gives me plenty of time to waver, as the hand of the bedroom clock ticks its way slowly to the hour. This is utter madness, I think, almost losing my nerve, but in the end the urge to see Henry is just too overpowering.

I open my bedroom door the barest crack and listen carefully. The volume of the snoring increases, so I risk placing one foot on the landing. Again, I wait and listen, poised to dash back into my room if necessary. After a few seconds, when I'm happy the coast is clear, I make my way to the stairs, treading to one side of the steps to avoid any creaks and moans giving me away. It's as though I've descended a mountain by the time I reach the bottom, my heart pounding so hard and fast I feel dizzy.

My coat and boots sit waiting near the door, but I still even now wonder if I have the nerve to continue. I've never done anything like this before in my life, always obedient, and toeing the line.

I steel myself once and for all. The wheels are in motion, steadily picking up speed, and now that I've set foot outside this door, it's become impossible for me to slam on the brakes.

*

I'd know my way up here blindfolded, but it's a clear and crisp night, the ever-watchful crags now bathed in a watery moonlight. At the top I can just make out Henry's cottage silhouetted against the midnight sky.

The handle of the back door to the cottage squeaks just a little as I open it. Some might think it odd, but nobody locks their door in Halifax. There's really no need, as you would be hauled over the coals by the townspeople, never mind the magistrates, if you were to take anything that wasn't yours.

I slip inside the kitchen, which is no warmer than outside. Henry will obviously be alarmed by someone in his house in the early hours of the morning, and it would be nice to have an alternative plan up my sleeve. But it's the only way, because if I knock loud enough to rouse him, the sound may well echo around the silent crags, waking the town. I'm certain he'll forgive me when the shock wears off.

Slipping off my wet boots I make my way through the parlour and up the stairs. There are only two more rooms other than his grandmother's up here, and the bathroom door is ajar. My hand rests on the handle of Henry's bedroom and I suddenly recall the last time I was here, when his poor grandmother lay barely clinging to life. I must squash that memory quickly.

I decide to speak the moment I open the door to try to minimise the shock he has coming.

"Henry don't worry it's only me, Bridie," I say, my eyes searching for him in the darkness. He scrambles to sit up and find the switch for his bedside light.

"Bridie, what on earth are you doing?" he asks, his eyes trying to blink away the sudden brightness.

"You scared the living daylights out of me. Are you alright?"

The bedclothes drop to his waist, so I have a glimpse of his broad chest underneath his half-buttoned pyjamas. I look away quickly, pulling off my hat and gloves.

"I know, I'm sorry, Henry, there was no easy way to do this. I'm fine, I just had to see you, that's all. I can't carry on being apart from you any longer, it's driving me to madness."

He runs his hands through his hair without a word, clearly still wondering if he's in the middle of a dream.

"I can't say I'm not over the moon to see you," he says, sliding his legs from under the covers, "but I have to say, if there was ever a harebrained idea, this is it."

My stomach is knotted, but I can't help a smile. He gets out of bed to stand gazing down at me with sleep-filled eyes.

"Well, mad as it is, you're here now I suppose, so if you're stopping then you might as well take your coat off, and I'll make us some cocoa. You look half frozen to death."

I ignore what he's saying, unable to wait a second longer after months of torment. Pushing my hands into his hair I bring his mouth to mine for a kiss. It's a kiss I could never have expected to experience in my life until this very moment. On and on it goes, his body so close I can feel every part of him.

"Bridie, don't," he whispers eventually, his longing for me pressing against my stomach. "Don't make me do something you might regret, I'm losing control."

131

"Then lose it," I whisper back against his mouth. "I've been starved of you too long, Henry, I need you, don't you see? You must know this is something I've given plenty of thought; I could never regret what happens with our love, not ever."

He tugs my coat from my shoulders to free my arms so I can unbutton his pyjama jacket all the way to his waist. He doesn't seem to notice my cold hands on his warm body, such is his passion. The fire is burning low in his bedroom, but it's enough to begin to thaw me.

I jump, startled when he suddenly drops his head back, letting out a moan of a tortured animal.

"What are we doing? This will ruin your life when it's only just beginning. You would be as hated as I am if this night was ever discovered."

I grab his face between both my palms to make him look at me.

"I'll run away with you before that happens. I don't want to leave my family and my job, but I've already decided there will be no competition if I'm forced to make a choice."

His shoulders drop as his eyes close.

"Do you really mean that? I would never ask you to make a choice."

"I know, and that's only one of the reasons I love you," I say, kissing him in such a way he can be left in no doubt about the truth behind my words.

He unbuttons my cardigan and dress and soon my clothes lay discarded on the floor. The same moonlight I sat under, gazing at the secret garden, falls on us through the thin curtains as he slides off his pyjama bottoms. He takes me in his arms, his warm, strong body a comfort as we fall on his bed, a tangle of limbs, his hand slipping to my breast. I gasp now, loudly, when his tongue slides around my nipple. How I want him, like a hunger, boldly taking him into my hand, so he moans into my hair. It already feels like something we do all the time.

"What's a man supposed to do?" he whispers in defeat, spreading my legs with his thigh. He slides inside me, so I cry out and he stops to look down at me in the blueish tinge of the room. I don't want him to stop, not now, only pushing myself towards him, the sensation making me say his name over and over. I become lost in him, as I know he is lost in me, the rhythm of our bodies taking me to a new, yet strangely familiar place. The sensation grows to take me now to somewhere else, somewhere special where I have never been. I hear a moan and realise it's coming from me.

"Whatever happens I will always love you, Bridie," he says between breaths as he almost reaches the place he's searching for. I cling my legs around his waist, panting, muttering how I love him into his chest. He pulls away from me suddenly, so the warmth of him lingers on my stomach. I didn't want him to stop, but he did, still thinking of me.

I'm already changed by his loving. What just happened between us felt as natural as sleeping, as breathing, and I already want more of it.

We lay a while under the covers, his arms around me, our faces close in his small bed. He asks if I have any regrets, I tell him none and I mean it. I laugh when he asks if he'll wake up in the morning to this all being a dream. I was the one who thought of the plan and carried it out, yet the night feels unreal even to me.

Eventually he gets up to throw coal on the fire and stoke the flames. He disappears downstairs, and I take in the room that has the simple charm of a man who has little interest in material things. The only decoration is a painting above the fireplace of sheep grazing on the moorland—it looks as though it could have been painted near here—and one single photograph. It sits beside the clock on his bedside table, showing him with his grandparents in a formal pose, obviously taken at a photograph studio. We have one, everyone does, but his is somehow tinged with a sadness. Perhaps I'm imagining something that isn't there, because he's alone now, but I spot the sorrow sitting behind their eyes. Henry looks to be around thirteen, his thick, curls creamed and combed to waves, and he's wearing a suit and tie. He looks like a boy trying to be a man. I think now this description might sum up his entire life.

He returns with two mismatched cups of steaming cocoa, and two wedges of buttered fruit loaf.

"A just after midnight feast," he says, with a grin. This man is so endearing, asking nothing of anybody, and I wipe a tear away quickly at the thought as he rejoins me in bed.

I will not spoil this precious night with sad thoughts. Soon enough I must return home, but for now I can laze in bed with the man I have been aching to see. If I should lie down, I risk going to sleep, so we sit side my side like an old married couple.

"Henry," I say, in between mouthfuls of fruit loaf, "I'll try to come again, but I've thought of a plan for the New Year. I hope you can have patience and faith in me until then."

He turns to look at me, the moonlight highlighting his dear face. I already know what Christmas will be like for him, painfully aware this will be his first one alone. I truly hope though that it will be the first and the last.

"I'll tell you all about it next time, I promise, but I'm anxious to get home."

He rolls his eyes, saying, "Oh, so now you've had your wicked way with me, you're off, is that it?"

"Of course, I have no use for you any longer," I say nudging him, and he makes a grab for me to slide his arms around me and press his lips to mine.

In truth, I could stay here in this room all night, but he jumps out of bed to pull his clothes over his pyjamas, telling me that he'll walk me down the hill. For once I don't protest, glad to have the protection of the night.

We hold hands for the first time, and I touch the bench when we get to it, glancing up at him. His smile is bittersweet, a mirror for my own I imagine, filled perhaps with memories, and the dread of saying goodbye for some time.

At the top of the crag, I reach to kiss him under the cover of the bushes, hating the thought already of leaving him alone.

"I hope I dare do this again," I say, "but until then, please don't live each day we're apart thinking we did the wrong thing. Trust in my plan, it's a solid one, as I've had plenty of time to think it through."

There's no hint of a smile as he nods his head. I slide my fingers from his hand slowly, loath to release him.

I must not look back for so many reasons, only imagining him returning to his cottage to climb back into bed, and the warmth I've just left. I've already lost my bravado and wonder if it can return.

The house is still silent when I open the front door. I remove my things with barely a rustle before walking in my stockinged feet to the staircase.

"Ah, here she is. The Scarlet Pimpernel has returned," a voice hisses in the darkness.

I spin round, grabbing the dresser to steady me. Archie, just visible in the dying light of the fire, sits in his pyjamas and dressing gown.

"So, it looks like what da told me is true," he says, his words floating quietly from the direction of the table. The half of his face I can see in the gloom is glowering my way. I can't speak.

"The poor man was in pieces, wailing into his pint glass, and to think I didn't believe him for a minute. 'No, da,' I told him, 'Our Bridie would never stoop to that; you've got the wrong end of the stick.'"

I want to flee up the stairs as my brother gets up from the table, but my feet are rooted to the cold linoleum floor.

"Bridie, Archie, is that you?" my mother asks, switching on the landing light.

We both jerk our faces in her direction as she heads down the stairs in her dressing gown, her hair still in curlers.

"Go back to bed, mam," Archie says, standing between us. "Bridie thought she heard a cat wailing in the garden, that's all. I got up to see what all the fuss was about."

"I thought one of you was ill," she says, as we follow her back up the stairs. My hand shakes as it grips the banister. "Do you remember, you always went to Archie first if you didn't feel well when you were little, Bridie? Thick as thieves the two of you, always have been."

My fruit loaf rises to the back of my throat as we say goodnight to my mother on the landing. Those blissful days she talked about can never return now.

Against my better judgement, I can't help but turn to look at my brother, as he makes his way into his bedroom and his sleeping wife.

His set jaw and cold eyes chill me to the bone as he stares at me … and I will remain forever grateful that my mother put in an appearance precisely when she did.

Chapter 17

My father settles himself down on the settee with his supper. Tinned salmon on a Saturday night is my parents' little treat, but tonight my mother has gone to bed tired, no doubt because I woke her up in the middle of the night. Edyth followed her not long afterwards.

"Where's Archie?" I ask him. He and my father always roll in the door together after watching *Town* play football on a Saturday, then heading straight to the pub.

"He's having a word with one of the lads in the *Feathers*," he says, not bothering to look up from his food. "He said he'd catch me up."

I waited up as I've had a sense of foreboding all day, spending the afternoon in the garden to keep out of the way. I thought it highly unlikely that Elliott Frobisher would interrupt my Saturday afternoon; he has other concerns now, but to be perfectly honest, I wouldn't have cared less if he did. He has quickly become the least of my worries.

"He knows," I say.

My father drops the fork just as he's about to take a mouthful of salmon, and it clatters on the plate.

"How? How can he know, have you told him?"

"Of course I haven't."

I can't say more because that would mean confessing my midnight trip up the hill.

"Look, da, I just need to know where he is. I've had a peculiar feeling all day that something is afoot. I can't imagine him taking it lying down."

He shrugs, telling me quite clearly that my concerns are no concern of his.

"Well, that we agree on, he shouldn't take it lying down. Your brother has every right to do what he needs to do," he says. "I wouldn't blame him."

I don't care for his choice of words. Cold words that take my breath; that tell me the talking is done. I pull my cardigan tighter, trying to warm myself, and head to the kitchen window to peer from behind the net curtain into the darkness. The curtain falls from my hand when I see a trail of torchlight snaking up the crag side.

"He's heading up there, da!" I say too loudly, forgetting for a moment about my mother in bed. "And he's not alone by the look of it."

He appears at my shoulder, pulling up the net as though he doesn't believe me. Sighing, he turns his back to return to his seat.

"Well, Friar's had it coming. It was going to come out sooner or later, and it's only to be expected, if you ask me. If I was a younger man, I would have been heading up there with them," he says.

As he flops down on the settee to resume his supper, I wonder where my father has gone. I'm not sure why I should be so surprised after his behaviour of late, but I am still.

My legs tremble with fear but something else too; fury perhaps. I refuse to take my father's lead in sitting tight and doing absolutely nothing.

"One man against an angry mob; what chance does he have?"

My father's eyes remain glued to his supper, unaffected by the desperation in my voice.

"I'm ashamed of you," I say as I hurriedly pull on my boots and grab my coat. I slam the door behind me, but not before I hear a faint sigh escape my father.

Fastening my buttons against the biting wind as I make my way across the road, I can see the mob is almost at the top making me run like the devil is at my heels.

Please let me get there before they do something reckless, I think, a horde of drunken men is a load of loose cannons. By the time I reach the top, I know they've already arrived at the cottage, as the path ahead is in total darkness. I can't bear to think what they have in mind for Henry.

It takes another five minutes of running against the wind for me to arrive at the scene, but I hear the fracas well before. There's the sound of glass breaking and men shouting as I scuttle down the path to the back door. It's as though I'm walking into a medieval witch hunt.

When I arrive in the kitchen, three men are pulling Henry from pillar to post in his pyjamas. Whether he came down of his own accord, or whether they pulled him from his bed is something I don't wish to think about.

Archie has my father's old cricket bat dangling from his hand, and I race towards him from the doorway when I see it. The shards of glass from the door crunch underfoot; he smashed the glass knowing full well the door would be unlocked.

My brother is unable to hear me above all the shouting, but when I grab his shoulder, he spins around quickly enough, his eyes going from wide to narrow in one swift movement.

"I'd go home if I was you," he says, shrugging my hand away. "Get home, because you'll not stop me, and it's best you don't stay."

Smashing doors down, threatening violence—it's like he's lost his mind.

"Archie! It's me you're talking to … Bridie. I know you're angry, and I understand why you would be, but just leave him be so we can talk. Call the lads off before it goes too far, and somebody gets hurt. This behaviour surely isn't the answer."

"Bridie, please … just go back home," Henry pleads from the parlour, the material of his pyjama top ripped at the shoulder already.

I make a lunge for the cricket bat, but Archie swings it out of my reach. I stand firm though my stomach is heaving, knowing all I have to offer in this moment is reason.

"I'm not going anywhere, Archie, so if you do anything I'll be here to witness it. I hope you'd rather not have that on your conscience, despite how you feel.

My brother stares at me so long I start to perspire at the thought of what he might do.

"Don't you dare touch her, Foxcroft," Henry says, apparently of the same mind. "It should be you who goes home if you've any sense, before I tell the police what you did. It can all stop right now, and it should."

Archie turns his face toward Henry, lips curled in a way I've seen before. The others stop tussling with Henry, but still their hands stay pinned to his arms.

"You shut your face, Friar, whatever happened you brought it on yourself, you know you did," Frank Dyson tells him, his cheeks still puce from running up the hill.

Henry wrenches his arms free, rising to his full height, his face a cold iron mask.

"Even if you're right, did my grandmother deserve to be dragged into it? Terrorising us for years, making our lives a misery?"

"Come off your high horse, Friar, don't try to shift the blame to me," Archie says, as I keep my eyes fixed firmly on the bat.

"You went too far, Foxcroft, you and your gang of troublemakers here." Henry sweeps his arm in the direction of the three men. "Just leave, all of you, and let's get on with our lives."

How did he go too far? I don't understand.

"What does he mean, Archie?"

"He's a coward and a liar, you can't believe anything a man like that tells you," my brother says, the others grunting in agreement.

I'm clearly missing something, as my eyes flit between the two of them.

"You need to leave my sister alone if you know what's good for you; do you hear me? She needs a good man who deserves her," Archie says in a low, threatening tone that sends a cold shiver down my back.

Henry's face is twisted with anger, but even so, I can see he's upset by the look in his eyes.

"A good man, you say? Would a good man do what you did; would he pay us a visit last Christmas with the rest of his bother-causers here?" he asks. "These so-called good men were shouting and swearing, breaking windows, trampling the garden, I could go on. My gran … my gran wasn't in the best of health, but she took badly that night, and the doctor said it was her heart. Don't you talk to me about being a good man, Foxcroft."

My hands fly to my mouth. No, it can't be true, surely, I think, as I look around all the furious men in the house. Archie is shaking his head, eyes locked with Henry's.

I almost stagger to the table and sit on one of the chairs, placing a hand to my chest as Henry's words sink in. My heart is hurting for a different reason to Henry's gran, but the same man is the culprit.

"How could you terrorise an old lady, how could any of you? She's gone before her time and all because of you and your crusade to make this man's life a misery. She was all he had; don't you see?"

Archie hurtles towards me as his henchmen pull Henry back, keeping a tight hold of his shoulders, his top ripping further. Archie's face is only inches from mine, making me pull my head backwards.

"You can't speak to me like that after what you've done. You're nothing but a bloody tramp throwing yourself at this malingerer. Da's ashamed of you, and I know exactly how he feels, because so am I!"

He raises his palm but I'm too quick, using both my hands to slap it away with such force he stumbles against the oven, his jaw hanging.

"Do that, and you'll never see me again. I've been considering it; don't you think I haven't. You consider yourself the better person after what you've done! What will Edyth say if she finds out? Coming up here and hounding the living daylights out of two defenceless people. Henry stood no chance against all of you. Answer me this if you will, Archie, who exactly is the so-called coward in this house?"

His icy eyes hold mine more than a few seconds, our chests heaving. He turns and marches out of the kitchen door as I glance over at Henry. The men let go of his arms, and slowly trudge after my brother.

I want to run to Henry so badly but the disgust in me means I simply cannot let Archie off the hook so easily; he must *never* come here again and cause such distress. Running outside, I find him slumped on the wall, head hanging. His pals are with him with hands in pockets, swaying in the wind.

My brother has never raised a hand to me in my life, in fact we've never had a cross word until tonight. He raises his head after a moment or two. His stare, in the moonlight, is haunted. My throat catches at the sight of it.

"You don't understand, Bridie, you weren't there, thank god," he says, his tone almost as though he's moaning in pain. "You wouldn't be able to understand unless you'd lived through it. We lost so many lads, our lads, and when we came home, well, the betrayal cut deep and still hurts even now. We all feel the same way, every one of us."

I close my eyes to the pain in his voice. This all must stop tonight, no more pain that can be avoided.

"Deep enough to send an innocent old lady to an early grave, I wonder. This terrible bullying has gone on too long up here, I know that now. Such behaviour is not what I would expect from the big brother I've always admired and looked up to."

Tears are sitting in his eyes as he stares at me.

"And you're not the little sister I was so proud of," he says. He drops his head again. "I didn't know about his grandmother; I swear I didn't know. I thought she caught the flu or something, how was I supposed to know any different?"

"Well, you know now, and you have to live with it, like I do. Just go home, Archie. Mam will be none the wiser, and you and I can talk tomorrow when we've had a chance to calm down and think about everything that's happened."

He gets to his feet, unfolding himself to reach his full six-foot-two height. My handsome brother stares down at me, yet I don't recognise him. I'm sure he will be feeling the very same about me.

"You still don't get it, do you? There's nothing to talk about, and there never can be. We can't just forgive and forget because you're my sister and you tell us to. It doesn't work like that."

I barely reach his shoulder at my full height, but I still somehow manage to stand firm.

"Well, I just don't know where we can go from here then, Archie," I say quietly.

His eyes search my face for clues, when there are none. He will be waiting forever if he thinks I'll back down over this and walk away from Henry.

Finally, he looks away, gesturing with his head for the other men to follow him. Frank flashes me a hateful look on his way past, one that would have crushed me if I wasn't so fired up. It's obvious that Archie is the ringleader, the one calling all the shots. I would have had far more respect for him if he'd come up here to challenge Henry alone, man to man.

Archie grabs his discarded cricket bat, and the other three men pick up their torches, strewn on the ground and still glowing.

I glance over my shoulder at Henry, who's now standing by the back door, his hands hanging loosely by his sides. He's been keeping a watchful eye on us.

"You should come back with me now," Archie says, backing away from me. "If you don't, then da won't let you back in the house and you'll break mam's heart."

My eyes drop to the bat in his hand, and he swings it behind his back as though this will somehow make me forget.

"I don't think I can go back home and carry on as if nothing's happened after tonight," I say. "We've both done things wrong, Archie, not just me. The difference is that my actions were done out of love, not hate. I'll talk to mam, but there's no easy answer. Her heart will be broken at some point because it's impossible now for me to give Henry up."

I lift my chin preparing for his response, as Frank calls, "Come on, Foxy, you're not going to get her to see sense, you're wasting your bloody breath."

Archie sighs, shaking his head before he spins around to disappear into the darkness and catch up with his cronies. They will be discussing my wrongdoings the whole journey back to town, no doubt. I wait a moment to make sure they've left us for good, then pass Henry to head back inside.

He closes the door and turns to me, looking as weary as I feel, and there's still such a long road stretching ahead of us.

Amidst the shattered glass and broken hearts, we somehow manage to communicate a thousand words to each other ... without uttering a single one of them.

Chapter 18

I must speak to my mother. It's important she hears my story directly from me, not second hand from my father or Archie. I owe it to her.

It's five o'clock and she'll be up at six, blissfully unaware of the trouble that's unfolded overnight. Neither of the men will have woken her, I'm certain of that much.

Henry and I sat talking all night by the fire after we were left alone. The wind was howling down the chimney as he told me his tale and we drank mug after mug of sweet tea to try to calm us.

My love was strong, but now I'm certain it's been anchored securely to a man who nobody cares to understand. How it pains me, shames me even, to think about my own brother's involvement in this pitiful situation.

"Do you want me to come with you?" Henry asks, as I pull on my boots.

He's still wearing his pyjamas with a pullover, looking so young when he's turned thirty. I think of the ripped seams of his pyjama top hidden underneath the pullover, out of sight, but not out of mind.

"If I thought it would help, I'd snatch your hand off at the offer. But I know it will only fan the flames and make matters worse. Archie will be licking his wounds now he knows how your grandmother died, and the only saving grace is that he won't want Edyth to find out."

He ambles towards me to encircle me in his arms, and I lean my head on his chest. The softest pillow could not give me more comfort.

"I should have told you what happened before tonight," he says, looking down at me. "I wanted to, but I've never spoken about it. I still don't want anyone to find out the whole truth, somehow it would be worse than all this even."

I read between the lines.

"They won't hear anything from me," I say, studying the greyness of his face. I touch his cheek, and he pushes his face into my palm, closing his eyes. He leans to place his lips on mine in a kiss so tender, I catch my breath. We have reached a new understanding between us; we've lived a life since midnight and I will allow nothing and nobody to force us apart now.

"Just come back to me is all I ask," he whispers. "We'll work it out, I have some thoughts but now is not the time to voice them."

It's never the time, I think, as I wave to him, there's always something lurking to darken the horizon. I set off to retrace my steps back to my … house. Home has gone, I think again, the awful, sickly feeling in my stomach worsening still.

The house is asleep as I creep inside, the peace a mask for what lies ahead. I must sit it out and wait until my mother comes downstairs to put the kettle on and begin her morning routine. This morning, I save her the trouble, lighting the flame under the kettle, and setting the tray for something to keep my hands busy. Then I light the fire and sit on the settee until the door clicks open, as it's done every day of my life before today.

I must wait still until she's washed and dressed in her winter dress of deep green, with her curls brushed out from the rollers she wears during the night. My mother always begins the day ready for anything.

Exactly as the mantel clock finishes chiming the hour, she appears in the doorway. Glancing around the room, she stops dead when she spots me sitting in wait on the end of the settee.

"Bridie! What on earth's the matter; why are you still wearing your clothes from yesterday?"

The colour drains from her face as she stares at me, taking in my dishevelled appearance, my jaw as tight as a vice. I hold out my hands, and she rushes to take them gladly before perching in her chair.

It's as though we're about to start sewing a new quilt—those were the days—and I bite my lip at the thought.

"Well, thereby hangs a tale, mam, and I'm afraid you're not going to like it one little bit," I say, running my thumbs over her white knuckles.

"Lass, you're worrying me now. Whatever it is, just spit it out for heaven's sake. It can't be worse than what I'm thinking right at this minute."

Oh, if only I could be certain of that, mam, I think, I could watch all my cares fly out of the window.

*

"So, what do you think?" Edyth asks, opening the door of the kitchenette to take a peek inside. The piece of furniture, a staple in every home since the thirties, has been freshly painted in a cheerful red and white, the shelving and drawers lined with fresh brown paper inside.

Sitting at the scrubbed table, I take in the Yorkshire range filling most of one wall, similar to my mother's range, only bigger and fancier. We rarely use it as we have a gas cooker nowadays, but you can't sit and warm the cockles of your heart around that, as she often points out.

"I think old Mr Frobisher has come up trumps. It's like a new pin in here and everywhere else. Even the range gleams so it looks like new, and that will have seen years of cooking in its time."

She shows me a hint of a smile before joining me at the table.

"He said he'd make sure it was up to scratch before we got the keys," she says. "We were going to surprise you all at Christmas by telling you we'd found a place to rent ..."

Her voice trails away, too kind to mention that I am the one who has now spoilt the surprise.

"Well, it's yours until after Christmas at least," she says brightly. "You need a bolt hole, and I know you don't want to live over the brush with Henry. Surely your parents must be grateful for this, if nothing else."

I had plucked up the courage to ask Mr Frobisher if he had a property I could rent in the short-term. It was no easy task to broach the subject, and I was a bag of nerves as I sat with him in his office.

"I won't ask if everything is alright, Bridie, because clearly it isn't by the look of you," he said, sitting back in his chair. "I'm afraid I don't have anywhere at present, but perhaps in the spring. The latest vacancy has just been taken."

I hoped to hide my disappointment, but I know my forlorn expression will have given me away. I've only spent one night at home since Archie's encounter with Henry, and it was one night too many, a terrible atmosphere filling every room until I couldn't bear it any longer. I was so desperate to get out of the house this morning, even if coming into the factory was like jumping from the frying pan into the fire.

To be fair, my mother took the news better than I could ever have imagined, hiding well the body blow my revelation must have been. She listened without comment, her only hint of surprise when Henry's name was mentioned. Even then, she didn't stop me from pushing on with my tale. My mother is level-headed, and I like to think I take after her, whereas Archie takes after my father. I was expecting some crying and scolding at least, but when I'd finished, she just sat quietly with her thoughts for a while.

"Bridie, I shall ask you this only once and never again, so make sure you tell me the truth," she said.

I nodded, my heart beating too fast even though I had an idea what she was going to ask.

"Are you absolutely certain that you love him? I ask because you're so inexperienced, and you could easily mistake infatuation for love. By that, I mean tipping up your entire life so it's unrecognisable, because if you think it's hard this morning, wait until the whole village, and the factory hear of it. We could have kept it between the family for the time being, but your brother has put paid to that by firing up his cronies from the *Feathers*."

She shook her head, her lips in a cold line.

If only she knew the full extent of his actions, but she wouldn't be hearing about his part in the death of Henry's grandmother from me. As I told him, we have all made mistakes, and I know those in glass houses …

"I do, I can't help it, and I never saw it coming. I've never wavered in my feelings towards him, despite the beyond difficult circumstances. I think of him and his happiness constantly, and I know he's a man to be admired for so many reasons. I'm sure, mam, I've never been surer of anyone, or anything for that matter."

I dropped her hands I'd forgotten I was holding and ran my fingers through my tatty hair. I must have looked a state. "Part of me wishes it was someone different, to spare us the trouble it will cause, but with love, real love, we don't get to choose like that, do we?"

"My, how you've grown up," she whispered. Her gaze, direct and far beyond my eyes, searched my very soul, it seemed, before she sighed and got to her feet.

"Well, that will do for me. It's precisely how I felt about your father, and we've grown stronger through the test of time," she said, reaching for her pinafore by the sink.

"Of course, talk of love won't wash with your father and your brother, so you'd do well to keep out of their way for today until work starts tomorrow. All I ask is that you don't go up to the crags, not today, though I know you'll want to."

I did want to; how I did. But it was only a small request in the scheme of things, and I was anxious to not upset my mother any further.

"You'll be in the middle of us all, mam, I hate the thought of that for you."

"I can fight my own battles, Bridie," she said. "The way I see it is that we don't choose who we fall in love with, love chooses us. If a mother can't or won't support her daughter when she's done nothing wrong, then it's not right. I'll not rub their noses in it, because they have their reasons for feeling the way they do, but I'll not bow down entirely to their opinion either."

She rubbed my back when I flung my arms around her neck. I should never have doubted her support.

"Go up to your room, and I'll bring you your meals. They'll be going to the pub at twelve if they can face it, then you can come out for a while and see Edyth. Today's not the day for a slanging match when tensions are running so high, but a little distance won't do any harm either. Take some sewing to do and a book. It will be a long day—the longest—but at least you'll have some peace."

So that's how I spent the day, albeit without sewing and reading, I simply couldn't focus enough, but it gave me plenty of time to come up with a plan. It began with seeing Mr Frobisher first thing this morning.

"I shouldn't be saying this, but as I can see you're in a predicament, I feel I must," he said. "The one available property is to be rented to your brother and sister-in-law in the New Year. Perhaps you should have a quiet word with them," he said.

Though I was surprised by his news, I was also happy for Edyth, and even Archie for a second or two. A home of their own was all they wanted, and money has become less of a sticking point for Edyth this year, thanks to our employer's generosity. She will be giving up work when they move out, I imagine, which will suit

Archie. He hasn't been a fan of her working after they married, but he put up with it because he knows we like working together. He hasn't minded the money either.

"You know, Bridie, I see you as a valuable business asset nowadays," he said with a twinkle is his eye, "but I've always been very fond of you since you were a young child, when your father took the job as caretaker. I always thought he was a fine role model as a father."

I recalled how Mr Frobisher always had a cheery word for Archie and me when he ran into us in the factory yard as children, and how respected my father is.

My eyes held fast to his, and I knew then it was better that I confessed before the whispers reached him, as they inevitably would soon enough. My ears were burning as they say, and they still are—I'm the talk of the town.

"It's true, I do find myself in a difficult situation," I said, unsure how I might find the words to explain. This clearly wasn't the right place or the right person to be speaking of love with.

He stared across the desk at me, the compassion in his eyes taking me unawares.

"Then I am all ears. You might think me out of touch with the real world, but I assure you I've had plenty of experience of it in my time. I wasn't always the old man you see before you. Is it a matter of the heart?"

We have spent plenty of time together in recent months, but I was still uncomfortable at the thought of talking to him in such a manner. I took a moment to choose my words carefully.

"It is, very much so, but there's more to it than that. I must tell you that the gentleman in question is … Henry Friar, and the gossip will soon be rife that I'm seeing him, and I am. But it's far more than that for me, and for him."

To his credit his expression remained passive, not a hint of disappointment or even judgement on his part. It made me think of my mother.

"Ah, hence the urgency for somewhere to live outside the family home." He paused for so long I considered breaking the silence. I wondered then if his thoughts of Henry were as hateful as the rest of the town.

"You know, Bridie, I'm sure you weren't oblivious to my displeasure when I discovered my son had invited you to our home in my absence that Saturday morning. I was extremely upset with him. It took me by surprise, and I'm regretful now of how I dealt with the situation, especially as you witnessed it."

I had no idea where his words were leading. The heated exchange I had seen through the window as I left to return home, showed me exactly just how angry he was with his son.

"This is difficult for a father to say, but my son is a man who thinks only of himself. I confess that I lay the blame at my own door for this. After his mother died unexpectedly, I threw myself into the business as a way to cope with the loss, and regrettably I overindulged him in other ways. He's used to getting what he wants. Yes, I was angry with him for bringing you to our home under false pretences and, as you now know, he had no right to do so when he's still a married man."

Oh, the secrets and lies that are spinning around all of us like a web, I thought then. If only he knew his son had been blackmailing me too, and lied about being divorced. I wondered if he intended to marry me, which would have been bigamy, or if he wanted me to be some kind of mistress. Which would be worse, I wonder? But Mr Frobisher clearly had his card marked well enough and was battling with his own guilt.

"The main reason I was so furious is even harder to confess." He heaved a breath as I held my own, unsure if I was up to hearing it. "Quite frankly, I do not consider him worthy of you. I must make my point, and I trust this confession will never leave these four walls. The point I'm making is that I only hope this man, this Henry Friar *is* worthy, because it would be an awful waste if you found out too late that he wasn't the man you thought. Sometimes we might think ourselves in love, only to discover over time that it was a mistake. This is not an unusual thing to happen, particularly in our youth."

He looked beyond the top of my head for a few seconds, as though reliving a memory.

"My mother has the same concerns as you, sir, as does Edyth, and I do understand why. I can't predict the future; all I know is that right at this moment, I could run away with him and go somewhere nobody knows us to build a new life. I must tell you I've been seeing him quite some time, and my mind is made up." I swallowed down the tears until one finally escaped. "I don't want to run away, only because of my family and my job. I love them both, and I know my family are disappointed in me, but … but I don't know if I'm strong enough to face the people in the factory, and worse still, the town."

Snatching my handkerchief from my dress pocket I wiped my eyes, then pressed it to my mouth to try to find my composure. Sometimes tears come at the wrong time, but Mr Frobisher was the last person I wanted to see me weeping.

"Well, I think you have gone above and beyond the call of duty here at *Frobisher's* over the last year," he said after a moment. "I'm certain you will have worked many more hours at home than the number you were paid for. Perhaps a day or two to try to straighten out your situation might be just the thing you need. Have a word with your sister-in-law. I can always present her with the keys to her new house early."

My face dropped at such a considerate offer; it was a lifeline, and I grasped it with both hands. My head fell back, sighing at being given a short reprieve, the relief making me almost dizzy.

"Oh! Mr Frobisher, I can't thank you enough, really, I can't. It's so thoughtful of you, and I'll make sure I work even harder to repay you," I told him.

I was forced to be candid, and he came to my rescue when I had run out of options.

"In that case, I shall ask Jarvis to fetch Edyth upstairs and give her the keys to the property. It's been given a thorough spruce, as do all my houses when they are vacated. Then I think it best if you both leave by the rear entrance to minimise any fuss."

He studied me carefully with eyes so soft I had to look away.

"I will say this to you first however, if it should become necessary, I will feel obligated to mention to the factory workers that if it wasn't for you, we would not have the business we have today. This factory would have closed within two years, and even if it was fate or happenstance that saved us in the first place, it was your idea and hard work that created the turnaround in our fortune. They have plenty of reasons to thank you, not least in saving their jobs."

His words were heartfelt, but I couldn't help worrying it would only make matters worse if he did. My colleagues would think more than ever that I was his pet, adding yet another reason to resent rather than thank me.

"I will remain forever grateful to you, my dear, and I shall also consider it my duty to remind your father of these facts … when and *if* my hand is forced."

Oh, dear god, if you do that, then I may as well pack my things and leave on the next train, I thought, as he smiled his encouragement, and picked up the telephone to summon Mr Jarvis.

Chapter 19

Slowly but surely my strength is being replenished just by being in the same room as Henry. When we're together, I think us invincible.

"I've been up here worried sick. I was coming down to the house if you hadn't called today, no matter what you had to say about it. A day is like a week up here nowadays," he says.

His cheeks are flushed when I pull away from his arms to look up at him.

"Well, I'm very glad you didn't, as it wouldn't have helped matters at all. I promised my mother I wouldn't see you for a couple of days, to let the dust settle, which was only fair. We seem to have found ourselves a team of allies in her, Edyth, and believe it or not, old Mr Frobisher. I've been very busy in my absence."

His lop-sided smile flips my heart, as I head to put the kettle on.

"Now, why doesn't that surprise me?" he asks, fetching the mugs from the dresser. He places his hand on mine as he reaches my side. How I've missed just being in this cosy, little kitchen.

"We'll need a strong brew or two whilst I tell you everything that's happened since I was last here. You had better brace yourself," I say.

Just for a mad moment, I imagine us living together in the quiet isolation of this tiny cottage that now seems like a refuge. The tweet of lapwings and the moan of the wind is only occasionally interrupted by a tractor grunting its way up the crag sideroad. I must shelve the thought with the other daydreams that creep into my mind from nowhere. I must accept I'm not just another girl who met another boy, there's far more to our story. But we can't hide away up here forever, in shame.

Edyth forced Archie to speak to me after I moved into his new home. She discreetly went upstairs soon after they arrived, leaving me feeling like a sitting duck. I felt safe with her close by and wondered how I could suddenly be so threatened by my own brother. He was quick to tell me when we were alone, what I already knew: that he'd only agreed to come to keep his wife onside, not wanting to risk her discovering what happened to Henry's grandmother. He would never have stepped foot over the threshold with me in the house otherwise.

"Look, Archie, first things first, I shan't tell Edyth what happened up the crags. All I want is a quiet life, nothing more. I know how upset you and da are, but do you really want me to move away, because that's what will happen? That alone will cause a rift between you and mam, whether you want it or not."

He was sitting on one of the two chairs by the fire like a sulky little boy, staring at the floor, unable even to bring himself to look at me.

"Oh, you're a fine little coven, you three, all banded together against us. You more than likely won't have any choice but to move away. When you go back to work tomorrow, there'll be consequences for you, and Edyth. I can't believe you would put yourself between me and my wife, damn you. I'm only grateful that da will be safe enough. The men all know how disgusted he is with you, and think he's thrown you out."

He threw his cap on the low table and raked his hands through his mop of dark hair, so like my own in colour. Guilt made me lose my tongue, as I didn't have a leg to stand on with the points he'd raised.

"You've made a right bloody mess of things, you know. The ripple of trouble spreads to all of us, and I can't even defend you. Do you know how hard that is for me and da?" He sat forward in his chair, making me take a step backwards, my heart leaping. "For god's sake you're making us into monsters; I could slap you, I really could. That's not me, but you're driving me to it."

I sat down at the table by the window, words far from my grasp, and stared through the net curtains into the street. Everyone was hurrying to and from the shops, getting ready for a Christmas, that, for once, had barely crossed my mind.

"Do you really think I want all this trouble?" I asked him. "Truly, I've thought about everything you've just said and more, but I still stand by my feelings whether you bully me or not." My tone was deceiving, making me appear far braver than I was.

"You won't finish it then?" he asked. "Not even for the sake of the family."

"Would you finish it with Edyth in my position?"

He jumped to his feet, eyes on stalks, so I gripped the tablecloth. "Don't you dare compare my love for Edyth with what you think you feel for that … that b

...coward," he spat. He checked himself just in time, as he never usually swears in front of a woman.

Edyth appeared right at that moment, looking between us both, hands on hips.

"Well, correct me if I'm wrong, but from where I'm standing, it doesn't seem like you two have made much headway," she said, blowing out a long sigh as she stared at her husband. "I think it might be best all-round if Bridie stays here for the time being, Archie. The house is empty, and if you won't agree to it for me, then you should do it for your mother."

I looked down at my hands, upset that she was having to talk to him in such a way on my account.

"Come on," he said, "let's get home to mam and da, I've had enough of breathing the same air as *her* for one day."

Despite his cutting words, it was as close to an agreement as I was going to get from him. He held out his hand to his wife, and Edyth touched his fingertips briefly, then dropped his hand. It hung in mid-air, telling all of us a story.

"I'll let you walk your temper off if, you don't mind," she said. "In any case, I have one or two things I'd like to do here, ready for when we move in. I shan't be long."

As my stare floated between them, I thought then, this is what my mother was worried about. She hoped Archie and I wouldn't have a rift if he broke Edyth's heart. Yet there we were, living out her worst fears, but for different reasons.

He soon realised Edyth meant what she said, storming out of the house with a slam of the door to make his point. I was only too glad to see the back of him.

"Oh, Edyth, I'm so sorry for you and for mam, it must be horrid living at the house at the moment," I said, rubbing my forehead with a clammy palm. "I won't let this go on after Christmas for all our sakes; if leaving is the only way to restore peace, then so be it. My brother's right about one thing though, it will be difficult returning to the factory for us on Wednesday. Your name will be as caked in mud as mine.

"Sticks and stones, Bridie, sticks and stones are the only things that can hurt us. You would do the same for me, and just remember that time is a great healer. Don't you worry, the men aren't taking out their frustrations on us at home, they know better than that."

Platitudes aside, Edyth's calmness and good humour were a tonic, and in spite of everything, we shared a low chuckle. It was so freeing even if it was fleeting.

Then, as I went to stoke the fire and she popped the kettle on, I wished for the first time I was able to tell her what Henry confessed to me.

If I told anyone it would be my mother or Edyth, but it would mean breaking a confidence, and one that is far too dear to risk.

*

Recently, I've learned that people are not always what they seem. I include myself in this. Once, I could never have imagined I would go behind my family's back, but circumstances sometimes mean we behave

164

'out of character' and this is actually who we are. My newfound belief is that people's circumstances and behaviour go hand in hand.

Our character is determined as children. I now know that Henry's childhood was so very different to mine, which was one of innocence and security.

Henry is quietly confident, a man who minds his own business. I think that has always been his nature, reinforced through what happened in the war. Yet circumstances now force him to stick his head above the parapet and that must be so difficult for him.

I knew that Henry had lost his father in The Great War when he was only a babe in arms. Archie told me as much, but that was all the information I had. We only ever saw him with his grandparents, and as children we accepted this without question. The Friars were only in my thoughts fleetingly, which seems so strange now. To me, if not to Archie and his friends, they were little more than strangers; just the people who lived up the crag.

Until the war came.

I didn't know all the ins and outs of it, and what I did know was second-hand gossip mainly. The plain and simple fact, however, is that when the call-up came, and the young men of the town trudged off to war once more, Henry didn't go with them.

He wasn't the only one of course. Some were too old or failed the medical; some were in reserved occupations, such as mining or farming, and this is where the grey area of Henry's situation came up. The men just didn't see his smallholding as a proper farm, or him a farmer.

It wasn't long before rumours started spreading that Henry had stretched the truth and was refusing to fight. It was just about the worst thing a man could ever do.

But just like the ones who went to war, one minute he was there and the next he wasn't in our lives at all. He retreated to his own world and life with his grandmother at the cottage. He was only spoken of in hushed tones, people thinking it was a case of good riddance to bad rubbish. Nobody cared.

That all changed on the night of the trouble at the cottage. Now I know everything.

After my brother left us, Henry and I sat by the fire trying to recover from the shock of the confrontation, and the secret I had discovered. Without any need for discussion, I knew there had been a shift in how we felt about each other. It was almost as though our bond had become a bind.

That moment was when Henry took my hands, delving into the depths of my eyes. He told me I deserved to know why he had to suffer so many recriminations. I had made so many sacrifices for him, he said, and it was time to tell me the full story.

I had longed to know why he had never gone to war, yet suddenly there I was, far from sure if I was ready to hear it.

"It all began with a telegram," he said.

The mention of that was enough to unsettle me. The telegram was every person's dread during the war, and that little scrap of paper informed Henry's mother of his father's death in the First World War.

"Understandably, she was heartbroken, the same as so many women who were receiving the same terrible news across the whole country and beyond. However, I now know many women did not react in the same way as my mother.

All the information I have is from the recollections of my grandmother. She told me that my mother had been struggling to cope after I was born, as she was pining for my father to the point of obsession. She would read the newspaper over and over to try to keep abreast of the war, so much so, that in the end they had to stop having them delivered here.

Then, as though my mother had willed it to happen or had a premonition, her worst fear became a reality, and news came that my father had been killed. At first her grief was raw as you would expect, but she gradually retreated into herself to live in a world of her own. As the months went on, she seemed to become worse, rather than being healed by the passing of time. After two years had dragged by, my gran was at her wit's end."

He was stroking my shoulder, deep in thought, as I sat curled up on the settee beside him. I kept my gaze away from his face in the hope of making it easier for him to speak of a time he was too young to remember, but I knew still pained him.

"Apparently, the doctor was coming and going for those two years, prescribing one tonic after another to try to lift my mother's mood. Nothing seemed to make any difference to her state of mind.

By the time I was three, she was admitted to 'hospital' as my gran used to call it. It was a sanitorium. She'd come home for a while, but she would stay in her room, only coming out for meals, and sometimes not even then. I lost count of the times I was told my mother had gone to hospital. It would be weeks before she returned, only for the whole pattern to begin again. She was like a ghostly figure coming and going from the house, and I admit she scared me a little.

That way of life became normal, and it dragged on until I was fifteen. Then when I came home from the mill one night, gran was sitting at the kitchen table, ashen faced. She told me my mother had died. Sitting there, I was only relieved it wasn't her who was taken from me, and I feel ashamed of that thought now."

I stole a glance at his face, but I had to look away. Half his life he has been battling grief, and it was there for me to see. Oh, Henry, you poor, poor man, I thought, to carry such a burden alone, and for so long.

Nestling myself closer to him, his arm tightening around my shoulder, I listened to the pounding of his heart. A few moments passed before he was ready to carry on.

"My grandparents were devastated, and grandpa died less than a year later—gran always said he never recovered from the loss of my mother—and I took over the work here. I tried to fill his shoes as best I could. We just had to carry on," he paused, "we had to, because we had no alternative.

When I was twenty-one, along came another war. My pals who were still working at the mill were champing at the bit to join up, and I was just the same to begin with. Believe me, Bridie, if you believe nothing else, I was ready to go to war just like them."

There was no doubt I did believe him. Even if I hadn't, I knew it would have been difficult for a young man not to follow the crowd. We only want to fit in when we're young, we need to.

"I even set off to go to the town hall to join up one day, but by then, I'd read the list of exempt occupations. The word 'farmer' jumped from the page, and it hit me immediately as a way out of my dilemma. The thought of leaving her alone to cope with the chores; of fretting day and night for years about whether I might return. Bridie, I … I just couldn't do it to her."

I clutched his hand, sensing without seeing the distress on his face, reliving that time.

"I thought of nothing else for weeks, watching the others do their duty, full of bravado and fighting talk. The more I thought about it though, the more I knew I just couldn't go to war for one person, and one person alone.

That person, who was all I had and who had sacrificed so much for me, had lost her daughter, her husband, and her son-in-law. If I went to war and never came home, she'd be left with nobody to provide for her, let alone to love. She wasn't my mother, she was my grandmother, getting older and more dependent by the day. Of course, I explained some of this to my pals, but they were young men with little sensitivity, only gung-ho for a fight and putting Adolf in his place. They had no time for sentimentality, and in the end, I gave up trying to make them understand. When they knew I meant what I said, they slowly retreated from me, and what began as a bemused irritation steadily grew into hate. They saw it as a poor excuse to shirk my duty. I don't know, perhaps I might have felt the same in their shoes."

My hand tightened around his. I could only imagine how tortured he must have been to have his loyalties pulled in different directions. A long trail of breath escaped him before he went on.

"It wasn't so bad at the start when people were volunteering, but when conscription came in, I knew what people would say about my 'exempt occupation'. I knew it would look like cowardice, but still this wasn't enough for me to desert my grandmother after all she'd been through. I was her only surviving relative. Whichever way I turned, I was going to be tortured in one way or another."

I tried to picture that time, as we sat in the darkness of his parlour. Even after so many years have passed, he must still suffer the consequences of his choice.

"When did Archie and the others start to bother you and your grandmother?" I asked eventually, my voice a hoarse whisper.

He dropped his arm to lean closer to the fire, elbows on knees. I was cold suddenly.

"It wasn't many weeks after they all came home, full of anger and bitterness about what they'd seen and done. They resented me when I'd been 'picking sprouts and feeding chickens' for five years. I'd planted more food to donate to the town, only to be shunned and sent packing at the market. I was living with guilt beyond anything you could imagine, but so was gran because she needed me at home. We never spoke about it.

They started heckling through the letterbox and hammering on the windows to begin with. Then there was the odd bit of damage to the garden if they were particularly drunk. I foolishly thought it would fizzle out given time, and to be honest, I understood how they felt.

We tried to ignore it, but last Christmas, gran said she'd had enough. She went outside to challenge them before I could stop her. They thought it was me, and they lunged at her … so she was absolutely terrified. I saw them off. They were shocked when they discovered it was gran out there, so they scarpered quickly enough on that occasion. I came back inside, and that was when she had the heart attack."

He hung his head, rubbing his hands through his hair. "That was the beginning of the end of her. I'm so sorry you found out, Bridie, but your brother left me with no alternative."

My arms went around him then, and we stayed that way for a long time with only the crackle and hiss of the fire. The shame of my brother's behaviour was burning me the whole time. I was at home last Christmas, and we were celebrating his engagement. All the while he was secretly up here, wreaking havoc, and I hadn't got a clue.

"The worst of it now is that I've ruined my life here, and my gran has gone anyway. It's been so hard to come to terms with the way she died."

His grandmother has died, but now he's trapped here still because of me.

Then, I couldn't help myself asking the question I'd carried around for so long. I didn't want us to have to relive that time again, and felt everything should be out in the open once and for all. It was the only way we could move past it; I knew there might never be another opportunity.

"Do you know how your mother died?" I asked him.

He turned to me, eyes glistening, and tears stung my own eyes without even hearing his answer.

"She was having treatment for her depression, 'radical treatment' my gran called it, but it only made her a shell of a person. Her illness went from bad to worse until basic tasks like washing and eating took too much effort. One illness just led to another. Pneumonia caught her in the end, but gran said if it wasn't that it would have been something else."

He swiped the back of his hand over his eyes, and I tightened my arms around him. I so wanted him to feel that he wasn't alone any longer.

I don't find it difficult to understand why he made the decision to not risk his life for the sake of his grandmother when he had an alternative. Farm or no farm, it's an isolated and physical way of life up here. At her age, the loss of her grandson would surely have been the end of her after all she'd been through. He might well have sent her to an early grave himself.

"I just can't ruin my mother's memory, I owe her that much," he said. "I couldn't find it in me to tell the world my grandmother had to watch her daughter lose her mind for years, because of the loss she faced in the First World War. Even if I'd spoken of all she'd suffered, I knew it wouldn't make a blind bit of difference to how they felt about me and my decision."

I dipped my face to look at him saying, "I don't think your mother lost her mind. I think she died of a broken heart. I read about it once, and that's what happened, I'm sure of it, Henry."

Our eyes locked, and his lips touched mine as gently as a butterfly.

"That's such a lovely way of looking at it," he said then. "Now I know such love I ... I can understand."

As we held on tightly to each other, I could almost feel the sag of his body as he offloaded the burden he'd carried around for years.

I can understand well enough, but talk of love and broken hearts will not wash with the rest of the town. They would not think any reason valid enough not to go to war. But those same men and women should be thankful they have never been called upon to walk a mile in Henry's shoes or his grandmother's, for that matter.

As we walked down the hill that night, my brother was at the forefront of my mind. But still, I couldn't help thinking about what it took for Henry to tell me about his mother, when he'd never told another living soul.

To be trusted with such a secret was the greatest commendation I could think of ... and the greatest testament to our growing love for one another.

Chapter 20

I pay far more attention to the task in hand than necessary as I work. Edyth is by my side doing the same I suspect, because the spiteful looks I can see from the corner of my eye flying around the work bench are not for the faint-hearted. All I feared is coming true, and I've only had a small taste of it as yet.

We took the little used back pathway to walk to the factory so we could avoid the people of the town. Edyth was waiting for me in the half-light of the December morning as we agreed the night before.

My worst fear has been running into my father on his early morning rounds. I saw him, but he just ignored me as always, going about his tasks as though he was alone, when I know he felt far from it. The dread of that first encounter is over now, at least.

At Mr Frobisher's suggestion, we used the rear entrance to go up to his office before starting work. His son just happened to be making his way back to his own office as we reached the corridor, and he offered me a sickly smile as he closed his door. I wouldn't have put it past him to time it to perfection, so he could witness my moment of shame.

His father was waiting with a reassuring smile for both of us, even getting up from his desk to greet us. It was as though he was delighted to see us back at work after three days off. I could have wept with gratitude as Edyth touched my hand lightly. The one-year gap in age has seemed wider of late. She's the second eldest in her large brood, and her motherly gestures are a great source of comfort.

I walked towards the man I've come to see as my protector, and managed to muster a smile through tight lips.

"Good morning to you both," he said, as though greeting old friends. "I can only imagine how you're feeling today, but I've come up with one or two ideas that might ease the way for your return to work."

Edyth and I exchanged a glance, eyebrows raised at the thought of our troubles being on his mind at all.

"My suggestion is that you use the kitchen on this floor for your tea breaks and even your lunch, unless you prefer to go home then. There are always tea-making facilities available, as Miss Whitehead uses this kitchen to prepare for board meetings, and she will be only too pleased to show you around. I hope this might help your transition a little." He looked first at Edyth, then at me, so my breath caught. "However, let me be clear on one matter: if either of you feel threatened, in any way whatsoever, you must tell me immediately. I will not tolerate such behaviour on my premises."

His cheeks set on fire as he shook his head at such an idea, and I wondered then if I could bear to add 'snitch' to my list of wrongdoings.

"Thank you for giving our situation so much thought, sir," I said. "I think perhaps at least for today we will take you up on your kind offer."

"Well then, I shall let you face the music downstairs, but remember now what I said."

Nodding, we left the room under his watchful eye, then Edyth and I blew out our cheeks on the other side of the door. The day hadn't yet begun, but we were wrung out with worry.

All eyes tilted our way as we swung open the double doors to enter the factory floor. The lively banter and chattering ceased almost as if a conductor had silenced the music with a swift flick of their hand. Our boots tapped out an echo on the flags as we made our way to the workbench. For once, I was delighted to see Mr Jarvis appear from his side office.

"Well, get to work, what are you all gawping at," he boomed, and the silence continued as I grabbed the doll parts I needed from the baskets to make a start.

I cast a look at Edyth when the bell rings for break time, almost throwing the thirty-fourth doll of the day I'm working on down on the bench in my hurry to leave.

"Off to the ivory tower then," Mildred Foster says in a stage whisper as we pass. "You can't hide up there forever you know, we'll all still be down here … waiting."

Her cronies chuckle as my stomach rolls, feeling slightly sickened by the menace in her words, though I know it's only talk.

"Sticks and stones," Edyth whispers as we reach the stairs. "I think we should go home to see your mam at dinnertime. Your da will be doing his rounds while we're all out, so we'll not be disturbed." She stops on the stairs and looks down at me. "You know I've been thinking, Bridie, you might find it easier in the checking room downstairs. The girls there are new, and you've shown them the ropes, so they won't give you any trouble. I know you were keen for us not to be separated, but things have changed. This morning is proof of it."

Oh, and how they have changed. Despite Edyth, despite Mr Frobisher, I feel alone for the first time in my life. Without Henry I'm cast adrift. I must see him later, as my courage is failing, set to run for the hills.

"Thanks, but I can't leave you up here on your own, Edyth," I tell her. "I couldn't live with myself if I did that."

As I drink my tea in the top floor kitchen, I place my hand on Edyth's as a great wave of guilt washes over me, almost taking my breath away.

"God, I've caused you so much trouble," I tell her, trying to gulp some air before I cry.

She puts her cup aside, placing her warm hand on top of mine.

"You haven't caused the trouble, the situation has. It's completely different and you mustn't forget it." Her lips tilt upwards as she looks at me. "Anyway, you're worth it, in case you didn't know. But don't get too big for your boots."

I manage a smile as my eyes roam her pretty face, thanking fate and fortune that I have her as a sister.

We scuttle off at dinnertime, my mother dropping her butter knife with a racket on the kitchenette counter when I walk in the house.

"By, you're a sight for sore eyes, love," she says, drawing me to her chest. Her hug is like a balm for my battered heart.

"I don't think for a minute you've had a good morning, but at least it's over with now," she says, as I stay folded in the warmth of her arms. "It's a test; and when the drama has ended and real life reappears, you'll know how you truly feel."

I move away to sit by the fire, as Edyth stands with her back to the flames. The drama has far from ended, I think. This morning was only a taste of what's to come.

"Nothing has changed in relation to how I feel about Henry, mam, but I don't know how I can drag myself into that factory every day," I say, rubbing my hands to draw some blood back into my veins.

They exchange the briefest of glances, making me wonder if they thought I would fold at the first whiff of harsh reality.

"I know it's hard, but it's only the first day," Edyth says, sitting opposite me. "We knew today was going to be trying, but they'll soon get bored with us."

I keep my doubts to myself, as I'd rather not talk about it any longer, but I'm not convinced. The townspeople have long memories, and their treatment of Henry proves it. I'm sure I'll pay the price for good, whether I'm with or without Henry. There are still nine days until Christmas, and I swore to myself I would give it until at least then to see if the situation settled, if only a little.

I try to join in the conversation about Christmas decorations to help lift our spirits, but my bread and cheese sticks fast in lumps at the back of my throat.

"Why don't you trim the house up, Bridie?" Edyth asks as we put on our coats. "It will give you something to do, and you can enjoy them whilst you're staying there at least."

I agree, it can't do any harm, though it's the last thing on my mind. My mother tells me she'll come and take a look if I do, so that's an incentive at least.

We head through the garden to the back gate to return to work. Edyth shunts into the back of me when I come to an abrupt halt upon opening the gate. Mildred Foster and two other girls are waiting for us in the factory yard. I should have known they would be ready to pounce at the first opportunity.

"Alright then, Mildred," I say when I've recovered from the shock, "just get it off your chest whatever it is you want to say, and we can be done with it."

She stands, arms folded, tangerine lips in a sneer, clearly pleased with herself that she's managed to catch us alone. I considered Mildred a friend, but if I think about it, she's always had plenty to say for herself.

"You know, we've all been a bit sick and tired of you and your high-falutin ways this past year. You've certainly become the boss's pet with your big ideas. You're not so cocky now though, are you, Bridie Foxcroft? You've a nerve to keep coming in here to work. I'd be on my way out of town if it was me, and so would the rest of us with any sense."

The idea is becoming more appealing by the day, Mildred, I think, taking a step nearer to the back door. She drops her arms to her sides, and I wonder what she's planning to do to me.

"Look, I just want to get on with my work if it's all the same to you. I'm not looking for any trouble with you or anyone else," I tell her.

The trio stand to one side, and I grab Edyth's arm to hurry past them. On my way, Mildred steps closer, spitting in my direction so it lands on my cheek. My jaw hangs in disgust as I stare at her; oddly, I would have much preferred her to hit me.

Edyth pulls me away before I can even think of retaliating in any way. She needn't worry, I will not lower myself to such a level as brawling in the back yard of the premises where I live and work.

As I wipe the spittle from my face with my handkerchief, I glance up to see the shadowy figure of Elliott Frobisher staring from the window of the ivory tower, as Mildred called it. His expression is hidden, but no doubt he will have been enjoying the little show, revelling in my humiliation.

I feel Mildred's eyes burning the top of my head all afternoon, and I count down the hours until I can leave. When Edyth heads home, I leave her at the door to walk up the crags and see Henry, heaving the fresh, cold air all the way. I have nothing to lose any longer in seeing him.

The next morning there's a great deal of chatter among the workbenches, but for once it's not about me and Henry Friar. Mildred Foster is nowhere to be seen.

Her seat sits empty, taunting me, but though the atmosphere remains frosty, the day is mercifully uneventful. It's much the same the following day, and by the end of the day after, the penny finally drops. I realise what has become of Mildred.

More than a little of me is relieved to not have to face her. But now my card is marked as a snitch amongst my colleagues, even though I never said a word.

Things are going from bad to worse and my comfortable and carefree old life is now something I dream about.

Will there be no end to the list of crimes the people of the town would be happy to see me pay for?

Chapter 21

It proved to be the perfect distraction in the end.

Henry and I stand, hands entwined, admiring our afternoon's effort. Between us we've managed to make his humble little parlour a sight to behold.

"It looks beautiful, though I say so myself," I tell him, as he slips his arm around my shoulder. The room is aglow with festive cheer, and it goes some way to lifting my heavy heart.

Earlier, we carried down a box of decorations his grandmother had stashed in the attic—a glorious treasure trove of glittering Wessel cup baubles and trinkets she will have collected over the years. Henry said he wasn't expecting to bring them down this year, having no appetite for decorating the house until my suggestion today.

He unwrapped the newspaper from the tiny Father Christmas with a sack full of toys made of tin. He held him up to the light as he recounted how he'd admired him in the toyshop window on a trip to Huddersfield. He has a tiny clock key in his back and when you wind him up, Father Christmas hoists his sack on his shoulder. He and his grandmother used to make a special seasonal journey for Christmas food and gifts each year to Huddersfield, and one Christmas Eve when Henry was seven, his grandmother told him they must take a detour. I can picture his face when she placed the ornament in his hands, and almost feel the sheer delight he must have had as a young boy growing up with so little. His eyes were shining the same today when he showed me it with pride.

"This piece is my new favourite," I say now, pointing to his childhood gift. "I think he deserves his prime position on the mantlepiece."

Henry brought in the smallest pine tree, which he'd found on the lea side of the moor, placing it in a pot of soil on a table under the window. The multicoloured Wessel cups now twinkle amongst the branches. I made a star of red velvet trimmed with gold braid scraps for the occasion, which we placed ceremoniously on the top of the tree as the finishing touch. It was such a happy, carefree moment between us that made life feel normal … if only briefly.

The roaring fire is adding to the life in the room, and I've lit more than a few candles now dusk is upon us.

Henry lowers his head to kiss me in the candlelight and I fall into him, thinking of nothing else. Resting my head on his shoulder, I indulge in a rare moment of peace.

"Thank you for going to all this trouble, Bridie. I was happy to give Christmas a miss this year," he says, stroking my hair from my brow.

The sorrow in his eyes makes me lead him by the hand to the settee opposite the fire to sit beside him. I lay with my cheek on his chest staring into the flames of the fire.

"I can feel her everywhere," he whispers. "Even in the newspaper wrapped around the baubles that her hands touched. Once the thought would have unsettled me, but now I find it comforting."

"I feel her too," I say. "I'm glad we've had today, we needed it."

Who can know where we will be next Christmas? This cottage has become our sanctuary, but this day is only a brief interlude from the reality we face.

I would prefer not to think about my family, the factory or anything else for a while. I look up at Henry's face, and want to kiss him, lose myself in him. His lips are trembling with all the emotion I too have coursing through me. How I need this man; he's mine and I am his, I think, as our kiss becomes more breathless. I want to show him my love and feel the burning love I know he has for me.

Grappling with his belt buckle I free what I'm craving. My hand caresses his hardness, making him drop his head on the back of the settee with a small gasp.

"Bridie," he groans, "I'm losing my mind over you."

I'm driven by an instinct now that takes over me, as I lift my dress and straddle him, my legs either side of his body. His look of surprise is intoxicating as I slide my way onto him, moaning from the pleasure of it. He unbuttons my blouse with frantic hands to free my breasts, running his hand over them so I move faster. Our hands now lock as we enjoy the rise and fall of my body, another new experience for me to collapse into.

"I love you, Henry," I whisper as our eyes hold. "Come what may, I'm yours, you must remember it when you need to."

"And I love you, oh, but I do," he says, his voice raising on the last word. I know he's about to release his passion and I want all of it this time. I just don't want this to stop.

My arms fall around his neck, breathing deeply into his hair. I drink in the scent of him, and how it makes me feel, before flopping beside him.

His face is taut when I finally come back to reality and look up at him.

"You know we're sailing too close to the wind. You should have stopped me, you were in control," he says quietly.

I know what he's saying to me, but none of this feels wrong. I'm in love, and I know without a doubt I will be with him always, come what may.

"I couldn't even if I wanted to," I tell him, "I don't know what came over me, but whatever it was, I don't regret it."

He presses his lips to my hand, saying, "I love you, Bridie Foxcroft. I understand now what love makes us do, some things are out of our control."

I am free with this man, I think, he asks nothing of me, which makes me want to give him more.

We drink hot milk with cinnamon by the fire and eat the ginger biscuits I made in his kitchen only hours ago. I *will* go home because I must, but I can't just yet. Once I leave this cottage, I will be out in the cold once again.

"Tell me of your Christmases at home, now you know a little of mine," he says, grabbing another biscuit from the pile.

I'm not sure I want to relive them at all. It will be painful, and I will feel as though I'm rubbing his nose in the differences between our childhoods. I stare at him a second, but then I think it would be wrong to deny my past. It's part of who I am today, and I know he would never want me to.

I place my cup on the table and brush the biscuit crumbs from my hands, laying back down beside him.

"Our Christmases started early in December with mam, always a stickler for tradition, cleaning the house from top to bottom. Be it pulling out furniture or clearing out cupboards for a fresh start in the New Year, I think it's symbolic as much as anything else. I would give her a hand and I enjoyed it as part of the build up to the day. She always made the Christmas cake on 1st November without fail, and my job would be to add a drop of brandy to it each week. I used it as a countdown when I was younger and had less concept of time.

Da would buy the tree from *Baldwins,* the greengrocers, like most of us, and always on the second Saturday of December. Then he'd go to the *Feathers* while we trimmed it up and added foliage we collected from around here to the range. The finishing touch was always the new rag rug we made for the occasion, and we'd stand back to admire our work, just like we've done today." I throw him a smile. "By the time three o'clock came around, da was full of spirit, and not only the Christmas kind."

We chuckle together, but then the memory of him rolling in from the pub and twirling my mother around the kitchen when he saw the tree brings a sadness. I brush it aside quickly, as Henry is clearly enjoying himself, reliving the time with me.

"Christmas Eve saw us running errands like everyone else, collecting the huge turkey da insisted we buy for the four of us, and roasting the ham with cloves for hours in the range. It just had a feeling all of its own; you'll remember it I'm sure, Henry, despite everything, something was hanging in the air."

"I do remember," he says. "In fact, I think I preferred it to the day itself, which could be a bit on the dull side, if I'm honest."

His eyes glaze, recalling those Christmas Eves he will have had in this very room. The parlour could not be more homely now, and I hope it was then, even with the worry his grandparents must have lived with.

"I loved that it was always thick with snow this time of year then, just the same as it is today. On Christmas Day, after we'd opened our gift and had breakfast, Archie and I used to go sledging down the bottom end of the crag road. Nobody was ever around, and if I think back, it was like a winter wonderland of our very own."

I gulp the last of my cinnamon milk down before I start to weep at the thought it can never be that way again for my brother and me. The simplicity of those times is lost to me, and there's nothing I can do to change it. Henry and I must create new traditions of our own now, and build them layer upon layer, year upon year.

"The day continued in much the same way as it did for you and everyone else in the country, except we all thought it was our own special day. It was, in truth— we had our Christmas dinner with all the trimmings, played board games while da slept off the drink, then had the ham for supper with mam's fresh bread and Wensleydale cheese and chutney. Christmas night was the only time all year da didn't go anywhere, and only then because the pub was closed. We sat by the fire in the evening, and I was just so happy we were all together, and nobody was going anywhere else."

Henry places his hand on mine, his face softened by the firelight. "Now, that feeling is what I recall most, Bridie, to be honest. Real life is always suspended for a while at Christmastime."

Our eyes hold, my mind swimming with the nostalgia of a time gone by, which I took for granted.

The clock on the mantle chimes five times, and I know I must go before the top layer of snow freezes, making it treacherous underfoot. Soon we will walk past our bench until we reach the bottom of the hill, and then share a kiss as always. I'll trudge past our house on the way to Edyth and Archie's new home, and pray nobody will look out, or worse still, come outside. The winter darkness and snow have become another layer of protection, keeping most people indoors.

"I wonder what we …" Henry says now, cutting into my thoughts.

As swift as lightning I raise my forefinger to press it to his lips. If I don't hush his next words, I will be in no fit state to go anywhere … not for a long time.

Chapter 22

"Bridie, Edyth, can I have a quick word with you both before you go," Mr Jarvis calls from his office.

We're only a stride from the doors, almost out of the factory, so his simple request makes me close my eyes then glance at Edyth; I thought we'd finally made it to the end of the day. I've been longing just to return to my temporary nest to hibernate, either there or in Henry's cottage, for the Christmas holiday. My working life has been subdued but manageable since Mildred Foster was dismissed. It was a warning shot for any other would-be troublemakers. I've been counting down the hours to this moment, but now I am to be waylaid.

Mr Jarvis has his coat on, ready to go home himself, his bicycle clips already in position. Pinning his trousers, they make his legs look like matchsticks, too flimsy to bear his ample frame. He doesn't appear quite so overbearing for once.

"Mr Frobisher has asked if you both might join him upstairs before you leave. I must be on my way, so you can head up there yourselves," he says, grabbing his bicycle, which is leaning against the wall of the foyer. It's a regular feature, a sign that he's in the building, and I don't think it's ever been out of position since I started work here.

I hold the door open for him to trundle passed, and I wish him a merry Christmas out of politeness. I have no idea who waits for him at home, if anyone, as I know so little of him. He nods, but doesn't return the greeting, making me wonder if he thinks there's no point in even bothering under the circumstances.

I can only hope now that it's old Mr Frobisher who wants to speak to us. Otherwise, I might just have to flee the building feigning illness, and deal with the consequences after the holiday.

In the end, I'm surprised when both father and son are waiting for us on the top floor. Four glasses of sherry and four mince pies sit on a silver tray by the fire.

"We shan't keep you long at all, ladies," Mr Frobisher says, "but we couldn't possibly let you both leave without thanking you for your hard work and dedication over the last year." He hands us each a sherry in turn, and I'm completely wrongfooted by the turn of events. Edyth's smile is hesitant, no doubt feeling the same way.

"My son and I shall remain forever in your debt." He raises his glass, and we do the same with round eyes. "Here's to you both, and not forgetting your mother's part in our success of course, Bridie."

His ruddy complexion makes me think this isn't his first glass of sherry today, as we thank him. I catch Elliott Frobisher's eye as I sip from the sherry schooner, but my eyes flutter away before they've even had a chance to land.

"I must reiterate my father's toast," he says quietly. "This time last year we were looking at a very different future for the factory."

His tone is almost amenable, and I wonder if he too has been enjoying more than a little festive spirit this afternoon.

"It has been quite a year," I say, my cheeks on fire, less from the sherry and more from the attention. "I'm relieved that between us we've managed to secure the future of the factory, and hopefully for many years to come."

"I do hope so," Mr Frobisher says. "We're especially grateful, as it's been such a trying time for you both these last weeks. I wish for better things in the New Year for you, and I haven't forgotten about you needing somewhere to rent once Edyth moves into her new home with your brother, Bridie. I happen to know of a lady on Potter's Lane who has a room to rent. The location is not ideal I know, but this arrangement will at least tide you over until spring, when the next property becomes available."

He's certainly gone above and beyond anything I could have wished for in trying to help me. Still, I can't help but think that springtime seems so very far away.

"I'm grateful to you, sir," I tell him, wondering now how to word my next question. I must know the answer, or I'll be fretting about it the entire holiday. "I must ask, however, does the lady on Potter's Lane know who would like to rent her room?"

The shame I carry will land on her doorstep along with me, should I choose to take the vacancy.

"Yes, don't concern yourself about that, Bridie. The lady has been fully briefed on the situation, and she assures me that you will be free to come and go as you choose. I'm sure the rent will come in handy, as she lives alone."

The option of a stepping stone is appealing, but how will it change anything? I sip the last of my sherry, knowing the arrangement will only stall the inevitable.

"Well then, we shan't detain you any longer," he says. "I wish you both a … peaceful Christmas break, and I will look forward to continuing our doll-making adventure together in January."

We return the greeting, but then in the doorway, Elliott Frobisher startles me when he touches my shoulder. His eyes are downcast as he asks if he might have a word. I glance at Edyth then at his father, who nods slightly only once. I somehow see it as a sign I have nothing to fear; I realise now his son would not be asking this question in the presence of his father otherwise.

"I'll head home, Bridie," Edyth says, already on the first step of the staircase. "I'll call with your mother tomorrow to see your Christmas decorations, like she promised."

We both wait like statues until the sound of Edyth's footsteps disappear, and then I must fight the urge to follow her. Elliott Frobisher gestures with his hand for me to go into his office, and I somehow still feel like a lamb to the slaughter. The room is smaller than his father's, but I'm surprised that today it looks very welcoming in the twilight of a snowy December day, with the glow of his desk lamp and firelight.

"Thank you for seeing me, Miss Foxcroft, I shan't keep you a moment," he says, nodding to the chair on the other side of his desk. He's in his shirt sleeves, his red braces festive, whether unintentional or otherwise.

"Well, where to start?" he says, rearranging his paperwork, still unable to cast his eyes in my direction. "I must tell you that I have been suffering a crisis of conscience these last months. I'm afraid I behaved rather appallingly towards you and … and I've asked you to stay behind today to extend my sincere apologies."

He finally raises his eyes to meet mine, and I make sure I keep my gaze steady, though my heart is beating too fast. I was not expecting an apology from Elliott Frobisher; what a peculiar end to the day this is turning out to be.

"Well, sir, I can't say it hasn't been a trying time, but it means a great deal that it was important enough to you to have this conversation," I say.

His sigh is dramatic, as though he's come up for air from deep water, before he runs a hand down his handsome face. He could have his pick of women, instead of setting his sights on me for reasons I have still to understand. His behaviour has been like a man possessed.

"I'm afraid an apology is all I can offer, though it doesn't excuse the way I treated you. I think now I may have lost my way for a while and my feelings for you were, shall we say, unexpected and … unsettling. I'm not sure how best to describe it well enough. I hope you can forgive me for not taking no for an answer."

I wonder briefly if his father has told him to speak to me, but dismiss the thought, as his regret is obvious. I remember how he witnessed the incident with Mildred Foster—he must have dismissed her of his own accord, and there was I, getting hold of the wrong end of the stick.

"I admit it will be a relief now to put it all behind me," I say. "I have one less thing at least to worry about. I wish you and your family a very happy Christmas."

He inclines his head in a gentlemanly way.

"And I hope your Christmas is better than you are no doubt anticipating. Next year will be better, I'm sure of it."

I stand up to make my way to the door, feeling his eyes following my every step as always.

"Before you go, I feel I must confess one last thing, so we can draw a line under the situation and move on from it," he says.

Oh, I should have known, I think, my stomach dropping to the plush carpet at my feet. I hold the door handle but don't turn around.

"I'm afraid I'm not in love with my wife. She's even more a stranger since she returned, but I will try my best to change how I feel, for the sake of our son."

This comment makes me spin around to face him.

"Mr Frobisher, you should not be talking to me of such things, it is none of my business. Please, let this be the end of it. You must let it be the end of it."

I expect a response of some kind, though he no longer scares me. I have so many other more important things to worry about.

Instead, he sits with the sparkle of tears in his eyes, the sorry sight taking my breath.

He loves me. I see it.

My palm flies to clasp my mouth, as I stare at him. Oh! He is a broken man, a man who suddenly seems on the edge.

"You think you love me, but you don't know me. It's impossible to love someone when you have not … not seen inside their soul."

One tear escapes, sliding to the papers on his desk, though he doesn't seem to notice.

"And you have seen inside the soul of your man up the hill?" he asks, quietly.

My silence is his answer. I have no need to rub salt into his wound.

I turn to tear open the door with a need to fill my lungs with cool, clean air.

A flicker of pity appears, despite everything, as I head down the stairs. He's trapped in a loveless marriage, and his affection, his love for someone else does not bode well for the future of his family.

But love does not make us act in the way Elliott Frobisher has; pursuing me, hounding me even, when I was unable to return his feelings. I would not have known this in the not-too-distant past, but I know it now.

As I finally leave the premises, I stare at the night sky cloaking the crags and can't help sympathising with his wife. Moreso, with his young son, who deserves to live a happy, loving life with his mother and father.

Many have spoken of their concern for Henry and me, unconvinced of our love … but unlike Elliott Frobisher, we, at least, have given our relationship, and our future together the thought it so rightly deserves.

*

The house is twinkling as much as the tree in the parlour window. I've had trouble sleeping, so I've used the time well to make one or two of my own homely touches to thank Edyth. I've sewn a lace tablecloth along with two cushion covers, and I've almost finished crocheting the second antimacassar for the back of the armchairs. The furniture was left by the previous tenant, and it's clean and serviceable, but I know the finishing touches will not be lost on her.

"By, it's parky out there," Edyth exclaims as she comes through the kitchen door, the cold following closely behind her and my mother.

I've already set the tea tray, so I just need to add hot water to the leaves in the teapot. My mother is bringing a Christmas cake for the visit. I've been cleaning and tweaking all morning to make sure the house looks perfect for their arrival.

"Well now, somebody's been a busy bee," my mother says, as she hangs her coat at the side of Edyth's. I can't help a touch of pride. It was so important for me to help make their new home as welcoming as possible in time for January.

"Wait until you see the parlour," I say, beckoning them into the room.

For a moment, it's as if this is my house and my family are dropping by for a Christmas visit to have tea and cake by the fire. Though the house looks picture perfect, it's still not enough to make it feel like my home.

My mother and sister-in-law stand side by side, muttering their compliments.

"Truly, it was no trouble, I enjoyed it." I say, running a hand over the delicate crochet of the antimacassar. "Anyway, it's given me something to occupy my mind."

Our eyes fly away in different directions as soon as the words are out of my mouth, so I could kick myself. I've brought us back to reality before we've even taken a seat.

"Well, it looks beautiful in here, Bridie," Edyth says, in a rush to put me at ease. "It's like a proper home, so cosy and festive, all ready for guests."

I bought the small tree from *Baldwins* and brought it home with my provisions for the week. I made sure I got there as soon as the shop opened when only one or two people were around who were too bleary-eyed for any shenanigans.

My plan is to spend Christmas Day with Henry. He's brought a small goose home from the town where he works for us to cook, along with all the other usual treats we look forward to this time of year. I've been squirrelling away Christmas goodies up there for a while, and we've made a pact to close the door on our troubles for one day.

"The tiny bows on the tree are so sweet. You're clever to have made them," my mother says now.

"Thanks, mam, it was a case of needs must, I couldn't have a bare tree. I'll leave them in a tin for you to use next year, Edyth."

Everything I'm saying is highlighting the position we're in. I can't do right for doing wrong, as my mother would say.

"I'll fetch the tea," I say, as they settle themselves in the fireside chairs.

"The cake is on the top of my basket," my mother says. "I've brought you one or two other treats and a little … a little gift."

Her voice breaks, and she looks away into the fire to hide her face.

"Great minds, mam," I say brightly. "I've made a little something for you all. I point to the four gifts wrapped under the tree.

I knitted mittens for my mother and Edyth and embroidered initials on crisp, white cotton handkerchiefs for my father and Archie. My mother will need to see how the land lies tomorrow to decide if it's a good idea to present the gifts. I somehow couldn't find it in my heart to discount them, it just seemed so peevish.

We take tea and chat politely by the tree for over an hour, tucking into our Christmas cake and cheese. Even the cake reminds us of the old traditions, and it's like trying to make merry whilst ignoring the elephant sitting on the other end of the settee. I'm exhausted with the effort by the end of the hour.

"Well, we must make tracks," my mother says, standing up and smoothing her skirt and blouse. She's made a special effort with her festive wine-coloured outfit, and my throat catches.

She doesn't add, "Before the men get home from the pub," but she may as well have.

"We'll call when we come to the shops the day after Boxing Day … if you're in," Edyth says.

"I'll make sure I am," I say, fetching the gifts from under the tree to place in my mother's basket. Lost for words, I can only watch them donning their outdoor clothes.

"Well then, merry Christmas, Bridie," my mother says, drawing me into her arms. She pulls away too quickly to dash to the back door.

"Don't worry, I'll look after her," Edyth says, pressing her lips to my cheek. "Merry Christmas, it will be better next year, you'll see."

Everyone keeps telling me this, but I wonder how exactly. I can't help thinking I'll only be exchanging one kind of sadness for another, if I'm not staying in the town next year.

"It gives me comfort that you're living with them at the moment, Edyth. I know mam will be glad of it too."

Edyth's sorry little smile is still on my mind as I wave them off and watch as they disappear down the back pathway to go home and try to have a 'normal' Christmas Eve together. The powerful sense of guilt and aloneness descends again, as I plump the cushions and wash the cups.

The loud rattle of the letterbox startles me from my thoughts. I dry my hands to see what could have been posted so late in the day. On the doormat sits a beautifully wrapped package about the size of a book. The gift is topped with a bright green bow, and I rush to see what it could be, as it looks so pretty.

There isn't a gift tag, but I admire the handiwork of the person who did the wrapping. I open the door. There's a handful of people walking in the street, but nobody who I know well enough to give me a gift.

Back inside, I pull the pretty bow and carefully remove the paper printed with tiny reindeers. There's a cardboard box and sheets of baking paper, and I lift layer after layer with anticipation. I'm touched by the trouble the giver put into their wrapping for me.

I carry on for a few seconds until an unmistakable smell escapes. It makes me drop the box on the floor like a hot potato, taking my mounting excitement with it.

The dog excrement in the bottom of the beautiful box stares up at me, filling me with revulsion and making me nauseous from the terrible smell. My hands are shaking, and I immediately think of Mildred Foster. I heave a sigh now, realising if it wasn't her, it could be literally anyone from the town; hundreds of people; hundreds of people who all hate me as I stand here right now.

As suddenly as a dose of smelling salts, another whiff of the terrible smell offending my nostrils brings me back into the room. The nausea I feel in my stomach turns quickly to fire, spurring me into action. Grabbing some sheets of an old newspaper, I fold the contents as though I'm wrapping fish and chips and push the parcel under my arm. I step into my boots and shrug on my coat, not bothering to fasten it, before stepping over the front door threshold. This is the first time I've left the house by the front door, and now there's nobody in sight. I'm only met with what should be a picturesque, snowy street scene on what should be the enchanted day before Christmas.

My rage grows with each step. Someone went to a lot of trouble purely to upset me. Whoever it may be, they would be smug and self-satisfied to discover they succeeded in their nasty intention.

I knew where I was heading before I even shrugged on my coat ... and the devil himself will not stop me now.

Chapter 23

The cigarette smoke hits me before the chatter, as I pull the door and stride into the taproom of the *Feathers*. There's little under half an hour left before closing time, and there will be a full house today.

Jake Thatcher, the landlord, spots me before anyone else, stopping mid-pull of the pint in his hand. His jaw swings, so the men at the bar look over their shoulder to see who or what Jake is staring at in such a way. It's an unsaid rule that women do not use the taproom, let alone this woman.

Those at the bar stop talking, but the rest of the men in the pub are in full flow, some standing, some sitting on stools and backrests. Dominoes rattle on tables, and there are four men congregating beside the dartboard, one aiming a dart right at this very moment. All is as it should be in their snug little pub world.

My breathing is laboured as I look around, waiting for the whispers and nudges to flow through the room and call a halt to proceedings. The newspaper parcel is sitting in my hand, every part of my body shaking with an anger I have never felt before.

My father looks up, still clenching a set of doms in one hand, when Archie taps his shoulder. His cheeks turn puce as he begins to scrabble to his feet, the doms clattering on the table, but something in my expression, I think, stops him. He sits back down heavily, so the men around the table fall quiet. The next table takes its turn, then the next, until I would not be able to hear a pin drop in the silence of this taproom.

"You've some nerve, Bridie, what the hell are you doing here?" Archie asks finally, getting up from his stool. Like Elliott Frobisher, he holds no fear for me any longer.

"Sit down," I hiss. "I've got something to say, and you're all going to bloody well listen, the whole lot of you."

The men look between themselves, eyes wide, mouths open, as I hold the parcel in the air before throwing it on the bar.

"This was put through my letterbox only moments ago. If you open it, you'll find out soon enough what it is."

Jake is the brave one to open a corner before they all take a step back from the smell, muttering their disgust.

"A fine Christmas gift for somebody who's done nothing to nobody, don't you think?"

"Bridie, just go home," my father says, as all eyes turn his way. "This is neither the time nor the place for theatrics."

My anger has nowhere to go. It sits in the pit of my stomach still, fighting to be released.

"I would, da, but I haven't got a home, if you remember. This is exactly the time and place, because if you don't accept what I have to say today, then I'll be gone by the New Year. I'm sick of it and I'm sick of the lot of you more. I've lived and worked in this town for twenty-three years, and I've never put a foot out of line or brought trouble to your door. So, why would I do it now?"

My eyes roam the room as each pair of eyes drop to the floor when I reach them.

"That man up the crag who you all hate so much is a good man. I would not have anybody other than a good man and I'm disgusted how you've treated him. He was orphaned, raised by his grandparents who did a fine job, and all he wanted to do was to repay their love and care. He doesn't deserve such hatred."

Archie tuts, his lips twisted with fury as he stares at me.

"Oh yes, they did so fine a job, he shirked his duty when push came to shove," he says.

The men heckle in agreement as I whip my head in his direction, my face on fire.

"You would do well to keep your mouth shut. We know well enough that people in glass houses should not throw stones. It goes both ways, so don't you dare push me," I say.

He knows immediately how deadly serious I am, and makes the wise decision to say no more, only sitting down and taking a huge swig of his pint.

"Do you think Henry just decided not to go to war on a whim, that he woke up one morning and thought, 'I can't be bothered fighting for king and country like everyone else, I think I'll give it a miss'"?

He had his reasons; *good* reasons and I accept them. But more than that, I understand, as should you, that a person is entitled to their privacy. He should not have to tell you things, things that would pain him, just for you to give your approval. No person should. But if you can't take his word for it, then you should take mine."

I feel a hot tear on my face and wipe it away with the back of my hand, furious at it for appearing at the wrong moment. The fire in me is still burning fiercely, stoked by these men over many long months, so it's now like a blazing inferno.

"My hand has been forced and I've come here today to tell you to leave us in peace, nothing more. But if you can't, then I'll have no alternative but to move away. I'd rather not, as I loved my life here and my job, but I love Henry Friar more, far more. He's worthy of such a love, by God but he is, and you should know me well enough to know I could *never* love a man who shirked his responsibilities, who cared for nobody but himself."

The men still can't look my way, but I press on, I've nothing to lose now.

"My family means the world to me, but da, Archie, if you don't at least accept what I'm saying to you, then you will force me to choose, and I would never want that. I don't think you would either. Mam and Edyth would still come to see me wherever I end up, so I'll never lose them but, believe me, they won't look at you the same again.

And when I say, 'accept what I'm saying', I don't mean for you to do it in the spirit of Christmas, and then change your mind down the line. For you to lord it over us and open old wounds the first time you're not happy about something. We're both worth more than that.

So, you can all be certain that I will be spending Christmas with Henry Friar at his cottage, and I will walk down the street and up the crag with my head held high from now on. If anything, and I mean *anything* happens to either of us again I will be gone, and believe me, I will never come back to this town. There would be nothing to come back for. You can go home and tell your wives and daughters just that, if you care to."

I stare at my father and brother, but they don't bother to look up. The edges of the room blur as I wait for some reaction, any reaction, but the room remains silent.

I turn on my heel to walk out, all the while foolishly hoping one of them will touch my shoulder or even say my name. Anything.

The stony silence follows me out of the door and into the quiet of a snowy, deserted street. I'm still hoping I might hear my name when I pick up speed, the falling snow chasing me down the streets and past the houses I've known all my life. I arrive at my front door with such relief I feel lightheaded.

Then I rush inside and slam the door shut with a rattle, just like Archie did when he left here, full of hell and disappointment in his sister.

I'm just in time for the flood of tears to arrive that make me fall onto the settee like a rag doll. They've been a long time coming.

The fire in me has been doused by the cruellest of rejections from the two men who I admired most in the world. Now I know in no uncertain terms that my course is set, and it points in one direction.

I left the house barely fifteen minutes ago, and the fire is still blazing away … yet I'm chilled to the bone.

Chapter 24

I stroke the wooden bench seat made especially for me with loving hands.

Henry made it just so I could enjoy my favourite view of my hometown. The love pours from every groove, every nail and if things were different, it would be somewhere we could carve our names and sit together in decades to come, reliving the memories.

My old home sits nestling at the forefront of my view as always, and I know I must look at it. I must face the bricks and mortar, but also the scene I imagine is unfolding inside.

In the house where I'm living there was no running downstairs this morning to open presents without a care; no sitting around a table full of laughter and banter; no warm, rosy glow. I know it will be just the same there.

But if yesterday is to mean anything at all, then today is a time for coming to terms with my future and taking the first step towards it.

That first step will take me to the top of the crag to spend my first Christmas Day with my love. Without his grandmother it will be so difficult for him, and I can choose to make the day either better or worse.

My tears were still flowing when I fell asleep last night—a Christmas Eve of nightmares—but I have no regrets about my actions. Now I understand that sometimes things must come to a screeching halt before you can slowly begin to gain traction and move forward. Even if it must be in a different direction. When I leave, it will be with a straight back and the knowledge that I have no unfinished business here. I did everything I could to sort things out *and* stay in my hometown.

The silence of the snow is a grounding force of nature, as I finally leave the bench seat to start my Christmas, and my new life with Henry. I'm wrung out, and just sitting quietly with him by the fire this afternoon, nothing more, will be perfect. I draw a breath of freezing air and continue the climb up the snowy hillside.

Then I see him.

He's been waiting for me, wrapped up snugly in his Sunday coat and scarf, eager to start our first Christmas. I close my eyes at the thought, then run the few yards between us until he grabs me, swinging me off my feet. His warm embrace is all it takes to grind my spinning thoughts to a stop.

"Merry first Christmas," I whisper into his ear. His lips touch mine, and I hold him to me so fiercely as though I might absorb all his quiet strength.

"What kept you? I've been looking down the hill since five o'clock this morning," he says, laughing. His face falls when he spots my swollen eyes, and I drop my gaze to the snowy path.

"Bridie, you're alright aren't you; you are staying for the day?" he asks, sliding his gloved palm around the back of my neck. I look into his eyes, red-rimmed also, but from the cold.

"Of course I am, silly, you just try to stop me. Come on, I'll race you to the cottage."

I have a head start, and he plays along, trying and failing to catch me, as though I'm a child, not wanting to spoil my excitement. There's time for reliving yesterday later, because I'll not have any secrets, but for now it's Christmas morning and there's fun to be had. Real life will descend upon us again soon enough.

The Christmas tree is twinkling in the window, and he's banked the fire so it's roaring up the chimney back. There's bacon in a pan ready to put a match under, and the whole cottage is once more that welcome haven where we can shut out the world for a while.

We cook breakfast together and put the goose in the range before we sit down to eat our bacon sandwiches. Henry seems as much at home in the kitchen as I do, but with an elderly grandmother to look after it's hardly surprising.

Raising my mug of tea I make a toast, "Here's to gran; I think she'll be smiling down on us today."

Henry's eyes mist, and he swallows hard. Her presence is all around us this morning, and better to face it head on than pretend otherwise.

"She'd be saying that you take your tea too weak for a Yorkshire lass, if she was here," he says, smiling through his tears.

"Oh, off we go with the quibbling already. Don't you be hiding behind your gran's skirts, tell me yourself if you don't think its strong enough, Mr Friar," I say, the corners of my mouth twitching.

His hand goes over mine, my heart flipping with love for him. If this isn't love then it's a poor do, and I'll get my coat, as my father would say.

Oh, I must not think of him and his many sayings today.

"This is nice," Henry whispers. "Normal, if you know what I mean?"

I know what he means exactly, it's all I ever wanted for us.

"What was that?" he asks me now, tilting his head to one side to listen more. I do the same, but I can't hear anything. I head to the window to peer outside, and a small gasp escapes me when there's a quiet knock on the door.

Henry tells me to stay put, but I can't help following him to the door, with Archie careering to the front of my mind.

It's not him; instead, Mr Frobisher stands on our doorstep with his driver, Joseph at his side, arms wrapped around a huge hamper.

"Oh, Mr Frobisher, what a lovely surprise. Merry Christmas," I say, a hand going to my chest. My employer was the last person I expected to pay us a visit. He's so smart in his fine woollen coat and a scarf of the deepest green. He lifts his checked trilby with a warm smile.

"Good morning, Bridie, Mr Friar," he says. "Forgive the intrusion, but I was hoping to find you at home."

He nods to Joseph who hands Henry the enormous basket. Henry and I thank Joseph at the same time before he nods and heads back to sit in the car.

"Well, this is most unexpected, but I'm very happy to meet you in person, sir," Henry says, placing the basket by the Christmas tree. "Would you care to come inside?"

"No, but thank you for the invitation. I shan't interrupt your Christmas Day long. I only wanted to give you this small token of my appreciation, and to ask if you might accompany me tomorrow, Bridie, to see your new lodgings. I know your brother and sister-in-law plan to move into their home early in the new year, so it would be nice to see you settled in by then."

"That's very kind of you …"

My voice trails away as I spot my mother and Edyth opening the gate. I watch them with my mouth hanging as they make their way towards the cottage.

Mr Frobisher follows my gaze, and they greet him, the smiles on their faces sitting somewhere between shy and pensive. My mother has a small cardboard box in her hand, and my eyes to go the box then back to her, struggling to believe she's here at all.

"Merry Christmas," I say finally. "It's so lovely to see you both. Come in out of the cold," I say, as though I do it all the time.

"Merry Christmas," my mother says, nodding first at Mr Frobisher then at Henry, who's moving his mouth without words.

"And felicitations of the season to you, Mrs Foxcroft; Edyth," Mr Frobisher says, raising his trilby once more. "Well, I shall leave you all to your day. Would it be convenient if I picked you up tomorrow at shall we say one o'clock, Bridie?"

"Perfect, thank you, I shall see you then, sir," I say, as he heads down the path towards his car.

Joseph has already opened the door, but before he gets in, he calls, "Oh, by the way, be sure to open the hamper today, there's something rather special on top for you."

With this cryptic message, he climbs into the car, waving as they drive away. I have no time to ponder on what this might be, as I'm eager to get back to my mother and Edyth. I can't help wondering how they've managed to get away with coming up here today.

"Well, I never. I didn't expect to see Mr Frobisher, of all people, this morning," my mother says. "They're not quite as fancy as that hamper, but we've come to give you these mince pies. I made them first thing. Best put them in the oven later to warm them."

I can't help a chuckle, saying, "Fancy indeed. We're very grateful for the gesture, mam, it means a lot to us, doesn't it Henry?"

His bright smile signals his gratitude as he thanks them.

My mother and Edyth exchange glances, and I'm about to ask them inside again when Edyth says, "Also, Bridie, there are others who would like to see you. We've come to pave the way, as they weren't sure if they would be welcome."

She turns and I follow her eyes now, almost dropping the box in my hand when I see my father and Archie step from behind the barn. They were clearly hiding like small children, as Mr Frobisher didn't appear to spot them.

Archie takes a step nearer, and I can't help myself putting a foot on the top step to place myself between him and Henry.

"Don't look like that Bridie, please. I know you've every right to, but don't. We're not here to cause any bother, we just came to give you this," he says, his quiet voice more like the one I remember.

He holds out an envelope, and I step away as though he's handing me a grenade.

"Open it, please, it won't bite," he says.

Somehow, I'm still not convinced enough to take it from him, only staring at the white envelope until he pushes it into my hand.

We must look a strange sight, all huddled around the little front door, but only my mother and Edyth are a welcome sight for us.

I turn and place the box of mince pies on the sideboard inside the door, glancing at Henry before resuming my place on the step.

I tear a corner of the envelope, my hands trembling, and still must peer inside to check it's safe to open. I pull out a card, a simple Christmas card with a robin in a cottage garden, much like this one. My eyes go to my brother as I open the card and read in his boyish handwriting, '*Christmas wishes from Mam, Da, Edy and Archie x.*'

This is a big gesture from my big brother. I extend my thanks, but he won't look at me.

"Wild horses wouldn't stop me from seeing my daughter at Christmastime, Bridie. These soft lads think they're in charge, but we know better," my mother says, her faltering smile breaking my heart.

I turn to Henry, who's smiling down at me now, an odd look in his eye.

"I have something to tell you about yesterday," I say.

His smile widens, startling me.

"Well, so do I and I'll go first if I may," he says, pulling me close to his side. "It appears we two have been of the same mind."

Our eyes meet, but somehow, I'm unable to return his smile.

"I know you said I risked making a bad situation worse by interfering, but I couldn't see how it could get much worse than it was. I had to try to do something, anything, to help, because I was going slowly mad up here." He shuffles his feet and glances at my mother.

"So, late last night I went to see your parents."

"You did what? I thought...." I begin to speak but Henry holds up his palm.

"That's when I discovered that you'd beaten me to it and had a word yourself, Bridie. Except, in your case, it was a brave word or two, with most of the town."

What is he saying? I thought he was the one in the dark, when it turns out it's me that has no idea what's going on. This Christmas morning has me all at sixes and sevens, I think, as I shake my head. My heart is pounding.

"What were you thinking, Henry, you could have got a fat lip or worse for your trouble," I say.

"To be frank with you, Bridie, I was past caring. We couldn't go on as we were, and I wanted to at least *try to* speak to your father, even if he wouldn't hear what I had to say for myself."

My father steps towards me now, his cheeks pinched from the cold air, but something else.

"Like the man says, he would have got short shrift only hours before, but what you said in the *Feathers* was still stinging. I was stewing on it after you left, and I didn't like the way it was sitting, not one little bit."

He hangs his head, so I can barely hear him when he says, "You were right, I should have trusted that you wouldn't give your heart to just anybody. I've been a stubborn old boy for months, and to think ... to think I nearly lost you because I wouldn't get down from my high horse."

Despite all that's happened between us, my hand goes instinctively to his arm, his obvious distress springing tears to my eyes. He's my father, and I've made mistakes, disappointed him too, and just coming here will have been such a gruelling decision for him to make.

"Da, will you come in, just for a minute?" I ask him.

Lifting his face, he stands up straight, dropping his shoulders with a sigh. When he looks at me, his eyes glisten, making a tear fall onto my best dress.

"Not yet, love, if you don't mind, I have so much to think about. I understand why you feel as you do and I'll give it the respect it deserves, but we need time. Not just me, all of us, including the two of you."

His words seem a step backwards from the hope I had in my heart only seconds ago.

"But will you *really* accept our relationship, da? I can't have you and Archie toing and froing with your opinion of Henry; of us as a couple. We must have a clean slate, or it will never work."

"Bridie, I've told you that I've accepted your feelings for Henry, and I shan't backtrack, you have my word. But softly does it, it's not right for us to force it."

That's something at least; my father saying Henry's name alone shows me the truth behind his words. Only yesterday it would have stuck in his craw to say it.

Archie looks at me, then takes a step nearer to Henry, who stands taller as their eyes lock. My brother holds out his palm towards Henry, saying, "We men all have some work to do. For my part I hope we can work together, not apart, for the sake of Bridie. I'd like this to start things off."

I wonder still if Henry will take my brother's hand, as it hangs in the air. I feel as though we six are trapped in a snowstorm, separated from everything else in the world as the snow floats around us.

Henry looks my way then grasps Archie's hand in a firm handshake. "For Bridie's sake," he says, expressionless and I know then that he too still has his own issues to work through before this truce can become anything more. My mother, Edyth and I share a small smile as we look between them.

"To a clean slate," Henry says, shaking Archie's hand then my father's, in turn. They make eye contact, giving me more hope of things to come. This is more than a gesture ... it's everything to me.

"Well then, that wasn't so hard now, was it?" my mother asks, attempting to lighten the mood.

Except we all know that really it was the hardest thing any of them has done since the war.

"We'd be glad if you'd both join us tomorrow for our usual Boxing Day fuddle at home, if you would?" my mother asks. "Just for an hour or two at teatime."

Henry nods and smiles my way, his eyes gentler than I've ever seen them.

"Of course, that would be lovely, mam," I say, accepting for the both of us.

Her shoulders drop with a look of relief, as though she's been holding them up against her ears for weeks.

"Right then, that's settled," she says, reaching on tiptoes to touch her lips to my cheek. "We'll see you tomorrow afternoon when you're ready." Her hand rests on my arm. "Oh, by the way, you caused quite a kerfuffle yesterday, Bridie. There was plenty of chuntering after you left the pub by all accounts. I've had a few visitors this morning, and I wouldn't be surprised if you find a few more people at the door as the day goes on. Enjoy your first Christmas Day … both of you."

I share a bright, genuine smile with my mother—the first in a long time—so happy to hear that the wish for peace extends beyond my family.

Edyth draws me into those strong, safe arms of hers.

"No more shame, you two. You would be a sad loss to the town, and they know it, and not just because you happened to save the factory, Bridie. I hope you will only look forward from now on."

I touch her dear face, and she gives me a shy smile. She was always my friend, who became my sister long before my brother stole her heart.

At the gate, my father turns, saying to Henry, "It took some brass neck to come to the house yesterday, lad, I'll give you that."

They nod at each other in the way men seem to do to communicate so much between them, and my father clicks the gate closed to join the others.

Swiping a tear from my cheek I look up at Henry, my father's words racing around my head.

"He's right you know. It won't work if we force it, and I think those are very wise words," I say, as we return to the warmth of the cottage.

But I know one thing at least, as I close the door on the world, it's safe to say Henry and I won't be needing to run away, not any time soon at least.

*

The house on Cragside, my old home, is once more a welcoming beacon of light in the darkness.

Henry and I sit side by side on the bench seat, his arm a warm blanket around my shoulders as we enjoy the view together.

"Well, that was the day, that was," I say.

We've had so many visitors it's taken us until evening fell to sit here. Still, this is my favourite time to enjoy the view.

"It's all down to you," he says, as the snow settles upon us. "If you hadn't found the gumption to give a hundred men a piece of your mind, then we would be having a very different day."

Laughing softly, I snuggle closer, savouring the newfound sense of peace. My dream for us to enjoy this simple pleasure for years to come is now within our reach.

"Thank you for making this seat for me, Henry. I'll never forget how I felt when I saw it. That was the first time I saw you in a different light."

He slides his hand over the seat saying, "I knew how I felt long before you did. Anyone who knows you will understand, but it's not something people mention. I love you because you're a one-off. I've known it a long time. I was never going anywhere, however difficult life became, once you'd decided you wanted me too."

Oh, how I wanted him, though it took me longer to know it.

"I lived each day terrified you'd disappear, Henry, and I never want to feel that way again."

Our lips touch lightly, moistened by the snowflakes, and I think this must be the most romantic moment a girl could wish for.

"Oh yes, we nearly forgot," he says now.

He pulls the thick envelope embossed with the Frobisher stamp from his pocket, the one we grabbed from the top of the hamper on our way down here. We both look at it until he hands it to me to open.

Inside is a telegram, and we look at each other, my heart in my mouth. My hands shake as I hold it between us to read.

It's addressed to Mr Frobisher, dated today, the time stating '*09.23*' precisely. I don't understand why he would have passed it to me of all people.

That is until I read:

I love the story of the young girl making the dolls for her sister. STOP. I bought one of each for my sister for Christmas. STOP. She was absolutely delighted. STOP. Merry Christmas, H.R.H. Princess Margaret. STOP.

Henry and I stare at each other and then back again to the telegram in unison. What have I just read I wonder.

"Surely not," I say eventually, reading the words of the short telegram again to be sure I read it correctly the first time. "Perhaps Mr Frobisher created it to cheer me up."

Henry chuckles softly saying, "I doubt it, Bridie, that would be an act of treason or something, surely." He studies it carefully before returning it to me. "Well, I never, it looks genuine enough to me. What a turn up, no wonder Mr Frobisher said there was something special waiting for us in the basket."

It's quite some time before we speak again, and it's only the cold seeping into my bones that finally makes me put the telegram back in the envelope.

"I hope you believe me now, Bridie, when I say that you're a one-off. It's not just your beautiful face that lights up people's lives."

His hold tightens around my arm as I stare down at the envelope, my head still firmly in the clouds.

"Good gracious, I don't think I will ever get over it. If I was Mr Frobisher, I'd place it in a gilt frame for all to see. I'd say we've been given the royal seal of approval, and that's worth its weight in gold. Wait until I show my mother and Edyth, they played such a big part in all this too."

The mention of their name brings us back to reality, and we sit quietly together a minute as I think of all that's happened this last year. I'm just about to tell Henry we should head home out of the cold when he says, "You don't need to go see the lodgings now though, do you? I thought you might be moving back home."

I place my hand on his thigh, staring down at the cosy, snowy scene with our house twinkling as much as the snow.

"To be honest, I'm not sure. I might still take up the offer if only for a while, as it will give us all some breathing space. In any case, I'd like to thank the landlady as she was prepared to give me safe harbour when nobody else in the town would have considered it. There's plenty to think about still." I glance at him now. "Anyway, we haven't spoken about you yet, you don't get away with it that easily. It seems you were busy yourself yesterday by the sound of it."

His coy smile, like so many things about him, speaks to my heart.

"About that," he says, "there was another reason I wanted to see your father, and I admit nothing was going to deter me."

I turn to give him my full attention, keen to know what was going on down at the house yesterday in my absence.

"I didn't think for one minute he would even talk to me when I set off." He glances my way, his icy breath leaving a trail that joins my own. "I went to explain I fully intended to pop the question today, and it was only right to ask his permission first as a mark of respect. I'd no idea then that you'd given him and everybody else short shrift."

He had it all planned out all along it seems. Oh, Henry, what a dear, sweet man you are, I think, as he stares into my eyes, searching for something, an answer perhaps.

I suddenly don't feel cold any longer.

"Well, Mr Friar, if that's a proposal, then I just want to know what took you so long? I was going to ask you myself on New Year's Eve if you didn't get your backside in gear."

As we throw our heads back, laughing together, it rings around the crags like church bells.

Our little bench has worked its magic.

Henry slips his grandmother's engagement ring on my finger. It's too big, but I don't care one jot, and I think now, no Bridie Foxcroft, you were wrong.

This is the most romantic moment a girl could ever wish for.

About the author

Jo Priestley is a Yorkshire author committed to writing historical fiction based on real lives and real people. She grew up with tales by the fireside, poignantly told by her grandmother, in her crumbling but grand house on the outskirts of Leeds, England. This created the perfect atmosphere.

She has been a professional business writer all her career, and now she would like to share the fictional stories that have been waiting in the wings, until the time was right.

After almost ten years of writing, eight books have now been published. They all feature women who have their own tale of love, life, and friendship to tell, and are set in and around Bronte Country. She is a proud member of the Society of Authors.

Jo considers the raising of five strong, kind-hearted daughters to adulthood her greatest achievement. Now she would like to commit herself as much to her passion for storytelling.

Printed in Great Britain
by Amazon

50603992R00131